# Spiritland
## Nava Renek

SPUYTEN DUYVIL
*New York*

LCCN: 2002109115

Acknowledgments: Thanks to Jessica Treat for her enthusiasm and support, Dan Coshnear for his editorial eye and keen insights, Chris O'Connell for his technical expertise, Tod Thilleman for his generosity, and to my girl friends for their humor and spirit. And to Paul Sweet: Thanks for the trip.

Spuyten Duyvil
PO Box 1852
Cathedral Station
NYC 10025
http://spuytenduyvil.net
1-800-886-5304

*For my father*

*D*ownstairs there's a bulletin board where backpackers and other travelers have put up notices to sell their clothing, sleeping bags, camping gear, and airplane tickets. They seem so desperate not to go home that they're getting rid of everything that makes their trips comfortable. Traveling seems to have become an obsession for them where the length of time away from home attests to their own strength and endurance. I don't feel that way. I'm still thinking about what I have to do when I get back to San Francisco, as if I'm just out of town for a few days and soon my old routine will start all over again. But then I remember that I don't have a routine, and I'm thousands of miles from home.

One notice catches my eye. It's larger than the rest and reminds me of those flyers I've seen hanging on utility poles when someone's lost a cat or dog, but the picture is not of a pet at all. It's a xeroxed photograph of a Caucasian girl. Her name is printed below the picture along with other personal information:

MISSING
CARA DURYEYE, AGE 21
LAST SEEN: BANGKOK
KNOWN TO HAVE ENTERED THAILAND JULY 17
WHEREABOUTS UNKNOWN. ANY INFORMATION, PLEASE CALL.

*Underneath is a series of numbers. One's for an Elaine Duryeye of Walnut Creek, California. The other is for a Don Duryeye of Mendocino County. There are also numbers for a private investigator and the local police. Then, jotted at the bottom in stiff handwriting, as if the sentence was scribbled by someone who wasn't used to writing the Roman alphabet, it says: "Overseas numbers may call collect."*

The copy of the photograph is poor, but, from what I can make out, the girl looks younger than me, maybe seventeen or eighteen, with closely cropped hair and a series of earrings running down the edge of her left ear. She's made no attempt to smile for the camera and all in all purveys a pissed-off attitude, as if she were reluctantly posing for someone whom she despises. I guess it's not a recent picture. Probably, it belongs to one of her parents who dug it out of a dresser drawer after hiding it there for several years, hoping their daughter would change.

Ben doesn't pay any attention to it. Whenever we pass, he just gives me a little nudge, indicating it's time to move on, but I always hang back to take another look. I just want to know who this girl is. How long has she been missing? Who is she traveling with? If only Ben would look at her more closely. Just having him next to me would protect me from the coincidence of it all, because being so far away from home has made me wonder what would happen if I just disappeared. Who'd want to find me? How would the search proceed? I think that's why I've decided to keep this diary, as if putting down words can keep me from fading away.

The first night we arrived in Bangkok, I had a dream; a nightmare really. I was asleep in our little cinder block room in the Siam Guesthouse when suddenly the air around me began to stir. The wind became stronger as it whistled over the laundry line, rattled at the wood slats covering the windows, and shook the door that Ben had purposely locked behind him before going downstairs to the bar. My temperature rose as a strange presence hovered above me, watching. Whatever was there was completely ethereal. It had a mind of its own and the power to go anywhere and permeate anything it wished.

When I woke up, the sheets were damp, my back ached, and my head felt as though it was stuffed with cotton wool. Not long after, Ben returned. He was drunk, and as he climbed into bed, I told him about the dream. "I tried to sleep, but my mind kept racing through all the different time zones we just traveled, so I picked up your guidebook. I've never really understood why anyone would want to know another person's impressions of a place before coming up with his own, but the pictures were colorful, and I just figured I'd be able to put the book down whenever I liked. The introduction told about the history of Siam, the different kings, and the fact that Thailand has never been colonized. Then there is an explanation about the language and money, but it's the chapter called 'Traditions and Cultures' that you should really read. According to the book, Thais spend all this time trying to pacify the spirits who they believe roam freely around the land. To trick the spirits, every family who builds a house or starts a business also builds a spirit house, a miniature of their original structure, which is meant to attract the wandering spirits and divert them from inhabiting the building made for humans. Don't you remember seeing those strange looking things on long poles on the way in from the airport? I thought they were bird feeders."

Ben pulled off his T-shirt and shorts and let them fall to the floor. His face looked flushed and excited, his brown curls matted to his forehead and neck. "Come on, Maddy. Can we talk about it tomorrow?"

"But I think one of those spirits visited me. It was this presence, really supernatural, kind of welcoming me to Thailand and telling me that now that I'm here, those kinds of beings have to be accepted."

"Yeah," Ben said, getting into bed and turning over to face the door. "And I met a Thai hooker downstairs who cried out, 'Oh my Buddha,' each time she laughed."

We stayed on Khao San Road, a street given over to guesthouses and restaurants that catered to low-budget travelers. For the first few days, as we trudged back and forth across four-lane boulevards, dodging motorcycles, cars, trucks, buses, and other exhaust-spitting vehicles, I imagined a glass jar being lowered down on us, capturing the smog and dust in an increasingly compressed area in which we had to fight each other for the last bit of air to breathe.

Afternoons were different than mornings. In the late afternoons, the red-faced *farangs* stumbled by half dazed from the sun, stopping to pick at the array of imitation designer shirts, jewelry, watches, and bootleg tapes being sold by vendors who set up tables along the edge of the sidewalk. Every half hour, a van full of travelers was ferried in from the airport and released in front of the stalls, where they were left to wander up and down the street, still wearing their knapsacks and winter clothing, looking like an exhausted tribe of Gypsies searching for a place to rest.

Slowly, we adjusted to the climate. Each morning I woke up to a glass of sweetened orange juice, fresh fruit, yogurt and granola, a breakfast which was offered at the restaurants along the road. Once the sun rose high in the sky, street vendors descended from all corners of the city. Old men and women squatted by the side of the curb next to baskets of barbecued chicken legs, marinated squid, beef *satay*, roasted corn, and a hundred other kinds of treats. Then in the afternoons when the temperature was too hot for anything savory, spindly men on tricycle carts rode around with sliced apples, skewers of pineapple, clear plastic bags full of pieces of papaya, and freshly chopped sugar cane kept on beds of ice.

At night we drank Thai whiskey or beer. Maybe it was the heat or the strangeness of the place, or the fact that one bottle of beer only cost about fifty cents, but I began to feel as if I could sail through the evening without any concept of time or any need to be somewhere else or to be doing something more important.

Ben never got out of bed until afternoon. Sometimes, I went upstairs to wait for him. Asleep, he was still, his long body wrapped in a starched white sheet. There were so many things I wanted to tell him, but we'd gotten to the point where we didn't need to speak. When we were sightseeing there was always something more exciting to see or hear, and the longer we stayed in Bangkok, the less we seemed to be communicating, as if the distance between ourselves and our old life was also pushing us apart. Maybe if we'd left something behind, a cat, a car, a garden or a house, we would have needed to discuss those things, but we didn't own much. There was always this unspoken issue, as if my life, so sedate and controlled, was holding him back from something more wild and unpredictable.

One evening, we sat in a garden café with a group of Brits. The girls had placed themselves on one side of the table and were gossiping about Asian spitting habits. The guys were sitting opposite them, with Ben and I bridging the gap. Across the way, a trio of German men seemed to be staring disappointedly at the lack of action they saw around them. Sensing that I was irritated at being locked in a circle, listening to one whining girl from Yorkshire, then a pouting Sloane—both of whom had pulled their chairs close to mine to discuss Thai toilets—Po, the bartender, sent over some lady-boys.

Ben had met these transvestites and cross-dressers a few nights before, and he started flirting with them. The English girls looked less than pleased as they glared at the lady-boys' bawdy behavior and watched their boyfriends, who hadn't yet caught on, follow Ben's example and carry on outrageously. As the scene played itself out, Ben and I withdrew to the background and let the momentum of drunken sexual attraction take over. Soon, even the Germans had wrestled themselves a spot in the conversation and were laughing and poking fun at the company.

Suddenly, one of the British girls pushed her chair away and stood up. "Well, I think I've had quite enough."

"Indeed," another sniffed, glaring at me as if I had

something to do with the situation. "Aren't you coming," she snapped at her boyfriend, using a tone of voice that didn't exactly give him much choice.

The lads rose obediently. The lady-boys got up too and began buzzing around, waving good-bye, and throwing kisses into the air. Then, in a swarm of departure, they all disappeared, leaving only Ben and me sitting in the court-yard facing the Germans.

"Zey vere really zomething," exclaimed one of the Germans. "Zey sure vere a lot of woman."

I looked at Ben, wondering when he would break the news. To soften the blow, he poured out five shots of whiskey. "Those girls," he began, after letting the liquor burn through our insides.

"Ve know. Ve know," the German cut him off. This time, his two friends smiled and nodded their heads also.

"You know?" I asked.

"Ja. Ja," they said excitedly. "Ve had zem last night. Zey vere *wunderbar!* How do you call it? Him? Her? Zey vere great! Like no other woman!"

Ben glanced at me and we both burst out laughing. That Thai whiskey was fantastic. After only a shot or two, the world became coated in a soft protective layer that made me feel as though nothing bad could ever happen to me. "They know," Ben repeated giggling.

"Wow," I sighed, too tipsy to get up from the garden chair.

Meanwhile, the Germans announced they were off to catch up with the lady-boys.

"*Guten nacht,*" I waved.

"*Ja. Ja. Guten nacht,*" they repeated, leaving us to make our way to the bar where Po was flitting about, pouring drinks, and laughing at his own jokes.

When we first met Po, he asked that we call him Michael Jackson in honor of his favorite American superstar. Now he explained that he came from a small island in southern Thailand and had learned English by working as a waiter in a five-star hotel.

"That's fucking great," Ben exclaimed. "You didn't need any goddamn book or tutor."

"No need," Po smiled. "Men want to take me out, buy me dinner, go dancing, and that way I learn the language. I go out with lots of men: American, English, Italian, German. I have many friends. Maybe one day we go out too. I take you to Royal Palace and show you beauty of my country."

I waited for Ben to say something, not knowing exactly what Po meant by "go out," but Ben was already agreeing enthusiastically.

The minutes passed in a vacuum as they did every day when the wide open space between breakfast and dinner suddenly disappeared and night fell. Soon, the street was nearly deserted, as it was every morning around four or five, after the vendors shut down their generators and hauled their wares back home. A streak of blue daylight began to emerge on the horizon, and Ben looped his arm around my shoulder as if to thank me for staying up until his favorite hour. With the constant flow of alcohol, it really hadn't been so hard.

Just as we were about to climb the stairs to go up to our room, a shrill cry came from the street a few yards in front of us. "Away! Away!" one of the lady-boys screeched as she ran behind the bar and pointed a red fingernail at a scruffy Westerner who was standing alone on the sidewalk.

At first I thought she was playing a joke, but as I

looked closer I saw that her lipstick had been smeared and her nylon dress was twisted around her shapeless body. "Tell him go," she pleaded to me as she ran to hide behind Po.

Her pursuer looked like a typical Khao San Road hippie: long hair, beard, rumpled T-shirt, drawstring pants. As he stumbled closer, I could see that his eyes were bloodshot and crazed. "You liar! You whore," the American cried.

Suddenly, a heavy object came hurtling toward us, hitting Po on the side of his forehead, then landing on the dirty floor. Po regained his balance and picked up the nearest empty bottle, smashed the bottom against the counter, and held the jagged edge out toward his attacker.

I waited to see if Ben was going to intervene, but he just sat as if he were watching some action movie, so I jumped off my stool and placed myself between Po and the hippie.

"Why are you protecting that whore?" the American called out to me. "You're just as bad as they are. Can't you see? They're working together."

"I don't care," I shouted back, unable to figure out why his anger was directed at me. "This isn't your country. You should leave them alone."

The American shook his head. "It's not right. She was going to rip me off."

"Go home and no come back," the lady-boy shouted, sensing it was safe to go on the offensive.

Slowly, the American turned away and stumbled across the street. Po made one more futile lunge with the broken bottle. A cut had opened up on his forehead and blood was trickling down his cheek. I looked to see what had hit him, and lying on the floor was a dog-eared copy of Lonely Planet's *Guidebook to Southeast Asia*.

Each day I was able to tell it was morning before I even opened my eyes, because of the rattling of bottles from downstairs as the guesthouse employees arrived and sorted through the garbage from the night before. Then, I'd wrap myself up in a sarong and make my way out into the courtyard to use the toilet. At that hour, the temperature was cool and the sweet smell from the hibiscus blossoms drifted up from the yard below. Sometimes, when I looked down at the open drain running along the side of our building, I'd see a family of kittens jumping back and forth over a trickle of water. The cats seemed so adorable bouncing up and down on their tiny paws, tails raised like arrows pointing straight to the sky. The trouble was, I usually went right back to bed. The evenings were too enjoyable to miss, just to wake up early the next day.

One afternoon, we were sitting at Sunni's restaurant watching some Nordic types next to us. Their knapsacks were packed, and they looked as though they were waiting for a taxi to take them to the airport. I actually felt sorry for them. They were going home to four hours of daylight and snowshoes.

Before our orange juice arrived, I glanced at the bulletin board to see if the picture of the missing girl was still there. It was. Nothing about her had changed; just another day had passed. "Do you think anyone from Khao San Road has called her family?" I asked. "Someone must have seen her by now."

Ben smirked. "Maybe she gets off on her little game of hide-and-seek. She could walk up and down the street everyday knowing we're all so sun-stroked, stoned, or just plain apathetic that no one will give a shit."

*Tuk-tuk* noises reverberated through the air. The drivers used those three-wheel vehicles as extensions of themselves, slipping in between stalled traffic and edging into pedestrians who strayed from the sidewalk. At first, I never wanted to ride in one. I was in no hurry to get anywhere fast, so there was no reason not to walk, but after a couple of days of traffic and ninety-five degree heat a ride in a *tuk-tuk* became more appealing. There were also public buses, but not enough to go around. As each bus got closer to the center of the city, the lines of passengers waiting at the stops became longer. Almost always when we took a bus, we ended up standing cramped in the aisle, clawing at the metal ceiling inches above our heads while holding someone else's baby, bag of coconuts, or crate of roosters.

We drank our juice and wondered what to do with the rest of the day. Outside, the road had become strangely quiet. Dust had settled on the street. The *tuk-tuk* motors had stopped rumbling. Even the Swedes had gotten up and moved to the front of the restaurant where they stood perfectly still, like cranes looking out into the distance.

We heard the chains and quick crunch of shackles first. Then came the grim faced Thai soldiers marching along, machine guns propped against their shoulders. Despite the fact that the road ended at the entrance to a police station, the only Thai police I ever saw were the ones in funny high-brimmed hats directing traffic while standing on top of pedestals in the middle of busy intersections.

I didn't look closely, or maybe I just didn't want to see,

but in the center of the procession staggered a figure in handcuffs and ankle chains stumbling to keep up with the guards. At first, I was sure I wouldn't know him. How could I? Of course, I assumed he was a Thai arrested for some back alley hold-up or swindle, but as the group moved closer I recognized the American who had fought with the lady-boy a few nights before, and I quickly slipped back into my seat. I didn't want to look at him or have him see me. I wanted that intransigent away from me, even if it meant he was led away in chains. Just by being American, I felt an ugly connection to him. What had he done? Where were they taking him? The police were parading him around as if he were a prize water buffalo taken to be slaughtered.

It had to be drugs. Drugs got Westerners arrested, but selling marijuana was as common as selling tobacco and everyone knew heroin was practically an export like the fake Chanel handbags and imitation Rolex watches that lay piled high on vendors' tables all along the street. Apparently, there was an intricate dance to be done. Many people were paid off. Lots of money was made. But, if you became a nuisance, the Thais had no trouble getting rid of you.

Posted on bulletin boards all along the road were letters from Western prisoners begging other travelers to come visit them in Thai jails. The inmates had no family in Thailand and wanted to talk with people who spoke their language. Nearly everyday the *Bangkok Post*, the English language newspaper, ran an article about some traveler whose parents were fighting to get their son or daughter transferred to a prison in their own country where conditions were bearable and there was less of a chance of contracting HIV.

After the procession passed, everyone seemed to return to what they'd been doing, but an eerie atmosphere lingered, as if people were trying to decide what their reactions should be. Should they rush back to their rooms and pour the quarter ounce down the toilet? Toss out the syringes? Or had the American just been the monthly sacrifice, and no one else was going to be taken in, at least not for the moment?

Ben sat down and finished his orange juice, making a long slurping noise from the end of his straw. "Shh," I warned. "Everyone's looking."

"I'm only drinking."

"Don't you think we should do something? We can't just sit here and watch him get arrested."

"What'd you think we should do?" he asked, as if the answer to that question would inevitably lead to the obvious response that we had nothing to do with the problem and should stay out of what was not our business.

"What's going to happen to him? He doesn't even speak Thai."

"They'll translate."

I looked down at the table and saw where other travelers had carved their names or initials: SVEN, L.B. LOVES E.C., MAN U. RULES! Detritus from the past. The Swedes hoisted their knapsacks on their long backs and turned out toward the traffic. Suddenly, I envied them and wondered if they felt relieved to be going home.

Many travelers left Khao San Road that day, as if the arrest was an omen of more trouble to come. For a few hours, the guesthouses sat empty, waiting for the next wave of travelers to come rolling through their gates. We decided it was time to go, too.

After packing, we took our bags downstairs to pay our bill. One of the workers, a pregnant woman lounging on the steps, shelling peanuts with her teeth, and popping the meat into her mouth, grinned as we went by and pointed to her swollen belly, then at me, indicating that she thought I should be pregnant too. I shook my head. Since our arrival, many of the older Thais seemed to see me as a vacant womb waiting for Ben to fill me with child. I was no longer sure that would ever happen.

Downstairs, Po sat on a stool hunched over his English dictionary. It was strange that no one was having an early afternoon drink. Usually, by one or two o'clock, there'd be a group of Australian surfers gobbling down bacon and eggs, their table littered with half empty beer bottles. "You go now?" Po asked sadly, as if he had never experienced guests leaving before.

Ben ruffled his hair, even though I told him I'd read that Thais didn't like their heads touched. "We're going to Chiang Mai."

Po looked wide-eyed. "Be careful. Lots of stealing men there."

I tried not to laugh. No matter where we told another Thai we were traveling to, in their eyes, it was never as safe as where we were, or where they came from. With that kind of advice, it was no wonder it'd taken us almost three weeks to get off Khao San Road.

The bill came to less than one hundred dollars. It was a shame to leave, but even Ben agreed that our routine had become tired. Every night, he stayed out until dawn, leaving me in the guesthouse to go to sleep alone. Then at 3:00 a.m., when I woke up in bed without him, I tried not to worry about where he was or what he was doing. Although I'd seen drunken and doped-up *farangs* stumbling home at dawn after having been stripped of their belongings, I knew Ben could take care of himself.

In the mornings, while he slept, I was left to wander around Khao San Road, waiting until he woke up. Most of the time I sat at cafés drinking coffee and listening to other travelers recount their tales of countries they'd been to like Indonesia, Nepal, or Vietnam. Some had crossed over to Laos or Cambodia or slipped into Burma. One daring adventure was topped by another. An Italian told about being detained with nearly an ounce of marijuana in his backpack while on a bus entering Malaysia. The police boarded the bus and asked the passengers to claim their belongings. Antonio had the choice of giving up his bag, hoping there was no ID to connect him to it, or getting arrested in a country where the penalty for smuggling drugs is death. He abandoned the bag and arrived in Penang with only his passport and wallet.

Fabian, a Frenchman, had crossed the border from Malaysia to Singapore where at one time the authorities used to stamp SHIT (suspected hippie in transit) into the passports of travelers who didn't have the clean-cut image they wanted their citizens to maintain. Barbers set up stalls along the causeway ready to give young men haircuts before they passed into Singapore.

Fabian told how he'd been traveling with a group of friends when his bus stopped for customs at the Singapore border. They all waited on the same queue, but when the time came to get their passports stamped, Fabian, whose straight black hair dangled below his shoulders, was pulled aside and all his belongings were dumped on a table. Knowing that he wasn't carrying anything illegal and would eventually be released, he waved his friends on and told them he'd meet them at the depot in Singapore. Unfortunately, when he arrived in the city, he realized that the bus made one giant loop through the center of town and there was no such place as a  central bus station, so he ended up back at the causeway again. That was the last he ever saw of his companions. He kept hoping that one day they'd turn up on Khao San Road, but now, four months later, he assumed they had left for Australia or Indonesia or flown back home.

Everyday, over coffee and while watching old videos like *Rambo* or *Splash*, I'd find the same group and sit and listen as they chatted on about the intricacies of drug dealing, gem smuggling, visa forgeries, and local prostitution. I mentioned the poster of Cara Duryeye, the missing girl, and they all laughed.

"That girl is missing to no one but her parents," Fabian said. "She's probably nodding out somewhere in Chiang Mai right now. A private investigator was around a few weeks ago handing out his card. I am sure he was making a whole lot of baht off that family. That's the hardest I've ever seen any Thai work."

A British girl named Gwen shook her head. "Thai women work bloody hard."

"Yes," Fabian answered, "if you call lying on your back all day working."

"You've tried it, I take it?"

"Well, I haven't exactly been on the receiving end."

Gwen shook her head in disgust. She'd been teaching

in a language school and lived with her Thai boyfriend. She told me she only came out to Khao San Road to be reminded of what wankers Western men were.

No one knew anything specific about Cara. Some suspected she faded into the conglomeration of travelers like we had, except, as far as we knew, no private investigator had been hired to find us. Antonio thought Cara had planned her own disappearance. Rick, an American, believed she'd been busted and was stuck in some Thai jail. I didn't know what to think. Maybe as a kid I loved those Nancy Drew mysteries too much, because I needed to know the end of Cara's story. That's when I realized that Ben might be content to drink his guts out in every city of Southeast Asia, but I wanted something more.

That evening, our bus sped along the flat highway that led out of Bangkok and into the countryside. Most of the passengers on board were Thais heading home from the city. The others were travelers like ourselves, rushing toward our next destination. I looked at the peaceful faces of the Thai men sitting across the aisle and wondered why I wasn't able to close my eyes and fall asleep like they had. Even at one o'clock in the morning I wasn't tired, and for a fleeting moment I wished I had a job or other responsibilities that would exhaust me.

Once we left the outskirts of the city, a loud Kung Fu movie was inserted into the video player at the front of the bus. Ben grumbled about having to watch the film all night. Then, in the darkness, he pulled out a bottle of Mekong from his knapsack and took a swig. It didn't surprise me that he'd brought it along, but the nice thing about being in Thailand was that nobody seemed to care. There were no sneers or disapproving looks. In general, that was the kind of attitude he expected from the world, but it was hard for me to ignore what he was doing.

"If you drink that whole thing, you're going to be sick," I warned, remembering that Mekong was the closest thing to sweet poison that I knew of.

"I feel sick right now," he laughed and turned toward me, pretending he was about to puke. "Loosen up Maddy. Don't act like such a fucking prude." Then he grinned just before brushing his lips against the back of my neck. I shivered and snuggled closer to him.

"The Thais sure have cornered the market on Freon. Did you know a few years ago, if a man had long hair, he wasn't allowed across the border from Malaysia to Singapore? There were barbers all along the causeway waiting to cut off ponytails."

"Well, that's sure one fucked up country. Why would anyone want to go there?"

"Fabian lost all his friends at the border."

"Fabian?" Ben snickered. "Yeah. I've seen him sitting around smoking his Gitanes. He doesn't seem too broken up about it."

"What would happen if I lost you?"

Ben kept silent for a moment and then took my hand. "Lose me?"

"Sometimes, when you're out all night, I wake up and wonder if you're ever coming back."

"You know I can't sleep like you do. That's just the way I am, but I'm not going to disappear. You're my girl. I'll always come back to you." Then, in the shadows of the seats we started kissing, and for a moment, I felt relieved, as if my world wasn't speeding out of control after all. It just seemed as though our lives were at the cusp of something big, but I couldn't figure out what it was. Alone at the guesthouse in the middle of the night, it was becoming harder and harder to remember why we'd left San Francisco in the first place. I liked traveling, and I loved being in Thailand. It was just that it seemed as if a thick curtain was coming down between us, separating us into two different worlds. I wished for some kind of magic pill we could both swallow that would make things the same again. "Let's just take a week off. We could stay in a nice hotel, watch CNN, swim in a pool."

His body stiffened. "A week off from what?"

"Cities are bad. Bangkok was so polluted."

"I thought you liked it there."

"I did. Now I want to relax," I told him and watched his pupils become opaque as the liquor worked inside of him. "Give me that," I said pulling the bottle away.

"Don't be stupid," he warned.

The crackling soundtrack on the VCR echoed down the aisle.

Soon, he loosened his grip and handed the bottle over to me. I grabbed it, unsure of what I was going to do next, but then I put it to my mouth. The familiar taste like rich molasses and pure alcohol burned my lips before streaming down my throat and scorching my insides. Then a surge of warmth rose through my body and my head became light.

C hiang Mai is not a big city, and there seems to be a lot less care about all things approximating the West. Hill-tribe people are dressed in traditional clothing. The music played from shops along the streets is no longer rock and roll. At the guesthouse, there are the usual assortment of travelers drinking coffee and picking at their plates of fresh fruit, but compared to the travelers we met on Khao San Road, these people seem much calmer. Maybe the excitement that comes with being in a big city lessens in the provinces? I don't know, but yesterday I finally sent a postcard home to mom. In Bangkok, I picked through all the cards with photographs of the floating market or of some glistening temple or shrine, but I just didn't know what to say to her. How can I explain the sights and sounds of a place so far away?

Ben never writes anyone. I envy that. When I ask him why he doesn't stay in touch with his family, he says it's too hard to travel when you're always looking back. I know he thinks I'm wasting my time standing on line to buy stamps at the post office, but I tell him that running away doesn't make your old life disappear.

I know why he thinks like that. Seven years ago, before he was eighteen, his flower children parents left him with relatives in Portland, Oregon, while they moved to an artist colony in Mexico. He claims to have forgotten all about them, but once we started living together he kept getting these phone *calls at our apartment. I was always able to tell when he was talking to his mother or father because his face would flush over and his answers became short and curt. He never really spoke to anyone else like that. Then, after the call was over, I'd stay out of his way, at least until he'd had a beer or two.*

During one of my early morning walks, I came to a fortress that is the Chiang Mai prison. The posters inviting travelers to visit the inmates were all over bulletin boards in Chiang Mai, and I decided to go inside. After all, anyone can take off their shoes at a temple or *wai* to saffron-robed monks, but meeting the prisoners was a way I thought I could prove to Ben that I wanted to see the *real* Thailand, just as much as he did.

The jail stood in grim contrast to the delicate teak houses and chirping birds everywhere else in that Asian landscape. Even in the sun, gloomy shadows fell against the boulders, making the walls seem somber and cold. By the size of the crowd of Westerners already lined up outside, I wondered if the prison held only Caucasians inside. We all stood there, contentedly waiting in line because time was of no consequence to us. We had nowhere else to go, no jobs, no pressing errands, nothing more important to do.

At ten o'clock, an iron gate swung open, and I followed the others as they trundled over a wooden bridge into a barren courtyard. Thai guards checked our paperwork and inspected our belongings. Nothing felt out of the ordinary. For all I knew, I could have been clearing customs at another international checkpoint.

An eerie silence hovered as we were led to a wire partition to wait for the prisoners. The air smelled funny, like rotten fruit mixed with sweat and dirt. Soon, I heard footsteps. That was when the heat of the sun hit me with all its might and I squatted to keep from passing out, my knees pressing up against my chin, my fingernails digging into the dry earth. One after the other, the prisoners filed in and paired off, taking seats along a narrow wooden bench. Each visitor seemed to have come to see someone in particular: the Italians were with Italians, Germans with Germans, and French with the French. The little groups looked happy enough. Except for the chain-link partition, the guards with machine guns, and the stone wall and barbed wire fence that surrounded us, we could all have been on a holiday picnic or family reunion. I was the only one standing alone, knowing full well that if I'd been in the United States, I never would have tried anything so foolish.

When I got up the nerve to look around, I examined the prisoners a few feet away. Their faces had the desperate expressions I'd seen in photographs of inmates in Nazi concentration camps. A pasty pallor had attached itself to their skin. Some wore cotton pajamas that drooped from their shoulders and hips. Others had on shapeless T-shirts and shorts that they must have worn each day and slept in every night. They didn't seem to have access to shaving equipment since most had grown beards that hung limply from their hollow cheeks. One of them smiled as he sat down across from a beautiful French girl. His teeth were brown and rotten, but the girl didn't seem to mind.

Each of the twelve prisoners already had company, and I wanted to slip away before anyone even noticed me, but as I was about to get up I spotted another group of men farther away. Nobody had summoned them, and the men acted as if they didn't care. One looked up and motioned to me, putting two fingers to his lips as if he were smoking a cigarette. I shook my head, hoping he'd understand that I hadn't brought any along. In response, he frowned and spit on the ground.

"Wait," I called out, hating myself for not realizing that on visiting day, cigarettes were the informal tariff for passing through the gates. "I can get some."

The prisoner looked as if he were silently tabulating whether it was actually worth talking to me at all, but then he nodded, and I knew what I had to do. Quickly, I turned and ran back through the gates, hurrying to a vendor I'd seen just beyond the prison walls. From a stand attached to his bicycle, the man was selling tiny packages of nuts, boiled sweets, and dried fruits. On the top row of his wooden display were a variety of brands of Thai cigarettes. Each pack was cheap, so I bought a few and hurried back to the prison yard.

The inmate was waiting for me and smiled as he looked over the packs I'd chosen, then asked who I had come there to see.

"I saw a sign at the guesthouse."

He laughed. "It's like a zoo advertising for customers. Every few weeks, the caged animals must be visited."

"I'm sorry," I mumbled, swearing that the minute I could, I'd get away from him. I didn't like how quickly I'd become a target for his scorn.

"I'm sorry, too. I'm sorry I was set up by the Thai bastards who decided not to give the police their weekly bribe. Christ! The Thais know about the drugs in the guesthouses. Sometimes I even saw people buy from the police. That's the thing about living in this country, no one knows the rules because the rules are always changing."

He stopped for a moment and searched behind me, as if he'd done his three seconds of conversation and was now looking for someone more interesting to talk to; someone who had thought to bring Marlboros or Camels instead of cheap Thai cigarettes. I wasn't so crazy about him either. His speech seemed like a stock harangue he must have given to anyone whom he came in contact with, but the more he spoke about his arrest and the injustices that followed, the more animated he became.

"Isn't there someone who can help you?" I asked.

He spat into the dust again. "Sure. The American consul comes out every few weeks, but there's not a hell of a lot he can do. The people in here are being singled out by a culture that's been created to lure us into breaking the law. Do you think I flushed myself full of junk before I got here?"

To tell the truth, I couldn't believe he hadn't. His entire body looked wasted. His bones stuck out like stretchers holding together a cockeyed canvas frame. He called over some of his buddies and generously handed out my cigarettes. "Tell her," the inmate continued. "When I came here, was I a virgin or what? Now look at me." He proudly turned over his arms, and I saw that the undersides were dotted with black-and-blue punctures where his veins had been perforated over and over again.

The other men snickered. "You were a real novice, mate," an Australian quipped. "Most of us have given up trying to find a good vein. If you ask me where I'd rather be incarcerated, I'll tell you right here because every Sunday, I don't have to look into me mum's weeping eyes.

Being stuck out here means it's not a question of whether the loved ones can visit, they simply can't, so no one's disappointed."

"Then who are all those people I came in with," I wanted to know.

"You see those bloody punters talking to those beautiful girls? They all just met a few weeks ago. When you're in here, visitors are all you've got. Them that once knew you don't care about you anymore, but others want to get to know you for very different reasons. Don't get me wrong. I want to get the hell out and go home, but if I can't, why not make the most of it, eh?"

Eric, the prisoner I bought the cigarettes for, made a face. "Fuck you! There's nothing goddamn good about being here."

No one seemed to be paying him any attention. Those men didn't need visitors; they wanted an audience to listen to them, just like the old men and women I met while doing field work for a sociology class, when I was sent from apartment to apartment documenting each geriatric's complaints about their slow crawl toward death.

Eric stopped shouting and pointed a crooked finger through the wire. "Tell them. Tell them! Why'd you come here?"

My mouth was dry, but I tried to answer. "I saw a sign," I choked, knowing that whatever I said was going to sound wrong.

"Never mind him," a Brit grumbled over Eric's shoulder. "It's good to see a new face. I can't stand talking to these bastards one second longer."

Everyone was angry, and I'm sure they had a right to be. I knew very little about their circumstances, and I wanted to listen, but their personal histories and their vying for attention were too much for me.

"We're not the only *farangs* in here, you know," the Brit continued. "There are men here who are too weak to sit up and too ill to eat. There's a fucking epidemic going around, or haven't you heard? HIV. We've all got it."

I couldn't think. All I knew was that I had to get out of there. I didn't want to desert them, but they made me feel as if there was now some ugly secret I knew about that could ruin the rest of my time in Thailand. How could I relax on a beach, trek into the mountains, or sip a cold beer in an outdoor restaurant, while these men were being held behind bars in a foreign jail? On the way back to the guesthouse, I thought about Ben and how unfair he was being. When we first decided to go traveling, *I* had been the one who suggested Thailand. I'd heard about the friendly people, the endless beaches, and inexpensive hotels. Why was it that he was now making me feel as though I didn't belong?

The first thing I did when I returned to the guesthouse was rip down all the signs asking travelers to visit the jail. Those men were criminals. It didn't matter that we came from the same country or spoke the same language, they hadn't respected the laws in Thailand; which couldn't have been too difficult to understand since the same laws seemed to apply to most countries around the world. It was just the severity of the punishment that differed.

Upstairs, Ben was asleep in our stuffy little room. That was no surprise. It was mid-afternoon, the worst time of day to be out. Usually, if I went outside before noon, I returned at that hour to cool off. But as I stared at him lying inert on the bed, I became angry that he had no idea where

I'd just been. I wanted shake him, wake him up and tell him about Eric and the other prisoners, see how he felt about me then. Instead, I tried to take a cold shower. As the tepid water hit my skin, I scraped at the prison dust covering my arms and legs and picked at the dirt between my fingernails. When I finished, I was exhausted and lay down on the bed to let the wetness evaporate beneath the rotations of the ceiling fan. From the open guidebook lying on the floor, I knew that Ben was thinking about moving on. He hadn't mentioned it to me, but I wasn't ready to go. Chiang Mai seemed like a place I could get used to, and although I felt strange about having visited the prison, I already wanted to go back; as if I'd been initiated into a club and now knew its secret language, but needed another chance to prove my proficiency.

That night, we sat in a backyard restaurant waiting to eat a fish we had picked out from a large tank located in the entrance way. I had suggested the restaurant as a treat. I wanted to tell Ben about my prison visit and try to convince him that I was just as adventurous as he was, but he seemed more agitated than usual.

"What's the matter?" I asked, unable to watch him fidget any longer.

"Nothing. Isn't silence a valid form of communication?"

I smiled, listening to him try to rationalize his rudeness. "Well, what is it that you're communicating?"

He sat up and rapped his chopsticks together. "Can't you tell? All I see of this country are fancy restaurants and expensive bars for foreigners. Why do I have to see everything through American eyes?"

"American eyes? I'm American. You're American. This whole country worships America. Maybe we picked the wrong country to go to."

I was worried this moment would come, but the fact that he was blaming me for his dissatisfaction didn't seem fair.

Just then, the waiter arrived with a bloated fish whose sooty eyes stood open like singed bullet holes. The sweet smell of the accompanying urn of jasmine rice filled the air. "I just spent an hour with a bunch of guys who were traveling like we are, and do you know where they ended up? In jail! Their vacation didn't exactly go as planned either."

He glared at me. "Why the hell did you go *there*?"

"I met an American. He said he didn't do anything wrong. He was set up. If you're not careful, you could end up like him too."

Ben looked incredulous. "What do you mean? I'm not dealing smack, or copping it from people I don't know."

Then it was my turn to stare at him.

"Jesus Christ, Maddy! This is Thailand. Did you think I was going to come all this way and not try the dope? That'd be like going to France and not drinking wine."

"Heroin? Is that what you're doing?" I didn't know what else to say. As far as I was concerned, he could have done whatever he liked, but I always thought he'd tell me if he was going to get involved in something that might affect both our lives.

On the way back to the guesthouse, I made sure Thai protocol was followed. Along the streets, you didn't see men or women breaking down unless they were drunken foreigners or whores. I wasn't going to give the people of Chiang Mai another reason to believe that Westerners were such emotional gluttons. They had enough drunk or stoned *farangs* stumbling through their streets already.

We walked quickly and soon reached the string of guesthouses and bars that was our safety zone. When I got upstairs, I threw myself on the bed. "How could I have been so dumb?" I cried. "It's so easy to see that this trip is breaking us apart. I've given up everything: my apartment, school, job, and you're on some kind of self-destructive quest that has nothing to do with me."

"I just tried it. That's all. You don't have to get so upset."

His voice sounded calm, which made me feel as if I were being the hysterical one. "You mean you won't do it again?"

He looked at me funny, as though I'd said something completely inconceivable. "It's great, Maddy." His eyes brightened, and he started talking faster. "You should try it. Someone told me there's this place up north where the stuff is pure and cheap as dirt. We could go up there for a few weeks. No one will ask any questions. It's what everyone does."

"But we just got to Chiang Mai. I don't want to leave yet."

He shrugged. "Then maybe I'll go myself. I won't be away long."

"And leave me here?"

"You'll be fine. It'll do us good, and when I come back, we'll be together again. I promise. I just have to see this thing through. What's the use of only going half way?"

"What if something happens?"

"What can happen? It won't be more than two or three days; a week at the most."

"And what'll I do?"

"You just said you didn't want to leave."

He took away the pillow I was clutching and placed his arms around me. I nuzzled against his neck, thinking of the two years we'd spent together and how I didn't want to lose him. It was only going to be for a few days. I'd be okay. It wasn't as if we were breaking up.

The next morning, he started packing. He packed meticulously. When we left San Francisco, he wasn't an exacting person, but each time we changed rooms I noticed how his packing became more and more precise. Every item was folded tightly and the correct space found, as if holding onto that order gave him some control over his life. If nothing else, I was glad to get rid of his ugly army surplus knapsack, the slimy plastic soap dish, his ragged sheet cover, and the crumpled copy of a Lonely Planet's *Guidebook to Southeast Asia*.

When all his belongings were wedged into a tight square, he sat down on the bed as if he were waiting for something else to happen. "Just like that?" I asked.

"Don't make it harder than it is."

"When we planned this trip, you never mentioned heroin."

Ben gave me one of his pathetic but comprehending smiles, the kind he used to flash when I complained about a boring lecture at school or how my mother wanted to know too much about me. I knew the smile meant he empathized, but as far as he was concerned those were situations that I'd gotten myself into. Then he came over and held me for a long time, as if my body gave him the sustenance he needed to carry on. "It's different for you. You have your life, college, your family. I don't have any of that."

"But where exactly are you going?" I asked, as I followed him down the steps and out into the courtyard, where it was buzzing with guests eating their breakfasts. I knew he didn't want to give me too much information, but he stopped when we were far enough away from the guest-house and no eavesdroppers could overhear what he said. "Believe me, Maddy, it's better if you don't know."

At first I didn't understand. I'd just spent every day of the last month with him. How could there be something he didn't want to tell me? But then I saw him differently. His pupils looked like black pinpoints drowning in a sea of liquid. His brown hair was greasy and tangled, his skin clammy, and even in the heat, he started to shiver. I'd seen that look before, nearly every evening when I came home from work and passed the strung-out junkies who stood outside the coffee bar next to our house and watched me as I fumbled for my keys to get inside.

I tried to understand what was going through his mind as he trudged off down the road, stopping a few yards away to wave a stiff hand, then hail a bicycle rickshaw to cart him the rest of the way to the bus station. How very Asian of him, I thought. When we first arrived in Thailand, he'd never have dreamt of stepping into one of those contraptions fueled by the power of a single human being peddling against physics. He probably would have tried to attribute that decadent habit to me, but there he was, proving how wrong his judgments against me really were.

*It's been five days. Where the hell is he? I didn't even bother to make him tell me exactly where he was going. What could be better than being here with me? Downstairs there are all these happy couples sitting in the garden restaurant, laughing, talking, their maps out planning their next destination. Why aren't we like them? We're supposed to be going south to the islands out in the Gulf of Siam. I know things will improve down there. I've always felt better near the ocean. Calmer. It's the rhythm of the waves, the softness of the sand against my back, the heat. That's where I want to be. Not up here in the hills. I guess when we planned this trip, we never considered that Thailand is a real country, with people who speak different languages and have another culture. It's not just one big long splotch of green on the world map.*

*Traveling makes you think about what's important, and Ben has always known his priorities. Not me. I have none. I'm like one of those sunspots you get before your eyes. One minute it's right there in front of you, the next, it's skidding over to one side, then back again, with no direction or reason for going one way or the other. Then you blink and your vision clears and the spot is gone. What's going to happen to me here? I feel as if I'm missing some vital body part. It's a void right under my chest where my heart should be; some hole that will never be filled and won't disappear.*

*I*'m not going to the police. Somehow, I know Ben's disappearance is self-willed, not the result of a mishap or crime, like his bus breaking down up in the mountains where no one has ever heard of a wrench, or him being kidnapped by Karen rebels and taken across the border into Burma. The police will ask too many questions. They'll probably find a way to turn their suspicions onto me. I don't trust them or anyone else around me.

Yesterday, I couldn't get out of bed. My body felt too heavy to ever leave the mattress again. When I woke up, I stared at the ceiling, wondering how I could go downstairs alone. Some days, I'm able to put Ben out of my mind, believing that he's just gone down to the corner to pick up some milk. I even imagine his bus creaking around the mountain curves and finally pulling into the station at Chiang Mai, then him taking a songthaew back to the guesthouse and my relief at seeing him walk through the gates.

There are plenty of other things to do to take my mind off waiting: people to talk to, sights to see, books to read. Most of the books have been left by other guests and are mysteries or true crime stories about atrocities that no one believes could ever happen to them. The plots are simple and easy to follow. Each event leads to the next, and the end is always guaranteed, not like traveling, where every day seems to bring me closer and closer to something unknown.

*In the evenings, I sit in the beer garden, glancing at the gate every few minutes, hoping Ben will come strolling through, knapsack slung over his shoulder, a goofy smile on his face, as if he hadn't meant to abandon me so many miles from home. All around are these content people chatting away, oblivious to what's happening to me. No one's bothered to ask any questions like what's become of the guy I checked in with, but now I understand that a single woman like myself is about as ordinary as the gaudy framed posters of Scandinavian fjords or Austrian gingerbread chalets that hang on the walls behind the reception counter at every guesthouse in town.*

Visiting day came again, and I couldn't decide whether to go. The way I saw it, if I went, I knew I'd feel as though I were cheating on Ben, giving my attention to someone else when maybe I should have been concentrating harder on finding him. But if I didn't go, I'd probably always wonder what would have happened if I'd gone.

The line against the wall wasn't as long as the first time, but most of the faces looked familiar. There was the French girl with her auburn hair and long legs who appeared as though she just stepped out of an advertisement in the pages of a glossy fashion magazine. Two Germans, dressed in oversized T-shirts and long muslin skirts, waited behind a group of Italians who were passing around a bag of peanuts. Some of them nodded to me, as if I were joining them on line at a bank or post office, not at some horrible jail thousands of miles from home.

The French girl turned to me as I took my place behind her. "Has your boyfriend been in long?"

I thought about Ben who I imagined was either nodding out in some dingy hut in the scrubby hills of northern Thailand or cuddled next to some Thai sex kitten he'd picked up at a bar in a country town, but I quickly understood that she was referring to one of the prisoners inside. "I don't have a boyfriend in here," I told her.

She smiled, as if to contradict what I just said, and asked: "Wasn't it you who came here last visiting day?"

I opened my knapsack to show her a carton of Marlboros. Before reaching the gates, I stopped at a shop near a string of fancy hotels where an old man sold me an expensive carton of cigarettes. I wasn't going to dole out pack after pack. I didn't have that kind of money, and I needed to control the rations just in case I ever wanted to visit again. The French girl threw back her head and laughed. "And you say you have no boyfriend? It will take no more than that to attract a man. *N'est-ce pas*?"

Soon the guards opened the gates and waved us through. Just as before, a small group of prisoners were ushered in from the courtyard. The Frenchman led the line. I couldn't help staring at his dilapidated condition, wondering how long he'd been inside. He ignored me and sat down opposite his girlfriend. Everyone else paired off as they'd done before. I didn't want to seem as if I were looking for anyone in particular, so I took a seat on the end of the bench and waited to see what would happen. A few minutes later, a second group of men appeared. At first I didn't recognize Eric, but he slid up in front of me, seeming not at all surprised that I'd returned. Without a word, I opened my backpack and pulled out the cigarettes.

"A quick learner," he complimented. "Next, you'll be bringing in sausage and Gouda cheese like the others. They can't help it. I guess we're a fascinating bunch of fellows, or maybe women are just attracted to men living in captivity?"

A bird began chirping from somewhere outside the yard, and he stopped talking long enough to listen to this manic bit of nature. Then he examined me more closely. "What's wrong? Has something happened?"

I wanted to tell him about Ben, but I was too embarrassed. How could my petty troubles compare with his more dire situation, although I thought my story might take his mind off his own problems, and maybe he'd even have an idea about what I should do.

He looked interested as I told him, and I might have even seen a twinkle of amusement in his eyes, as if my bad fortune gave him some kind of hope. "Well, where'd he go?" he asked.

"Farther north, I think."

"Smack," he pronounced promptly, a doctor proudly diagnosing some common disease. "Why else would anyone leave a beautiful girl like you?"

"He said he'd only be gone a week, now it's almost two."

"Don't worry. He's just nodding out on some excellent shit. He'll come back soon."

Then he shook his head. "This country changes you. When I first got on that plane in the States, I thought I was going to have some great mind-blowing experience, like when I returned I'd be able to see my whole fucked-up world differently and it would all make sense. I'd read these books about Hinduism and Buddhism, and I was ready to believe it all. How was I to know what was going to happen to me here?"

I wanted to say something comforting, like when his prison sentence was over, he'd be able to go back to the States and start over again, but I had no idea if that was true. He smoked his cigarettes and kept his eyes to the ground. If he hadn't been so skinny and jaundiced, he might have been attractive. His long blond hair was a rat's nest of tangles. At one time it must have been pulled back into a ponytail, but the elastic had never been removed and it had started fraying into his frizzy strands. When he glanced at me again, his eyes were cold, and his eyeballs bulged out of his emaciated face as if he had a pain he was completely unable to suppress.

His friends left us alone that day, but I could tell they were watching us from a distance. Somehow, propriety delegated that he was mine, and the time we spent together went by quickly. He talked about his adventures before his imprisonment: how he traveled through Thailand, then lived for months on the beaches in the south. Although he kept claiming he hated all Thais, his description of the life he led before he got busted made me wish that Ben would hurry up and come back so we could continue with our travels.

"There's this island in the Gulf of Siam," Eric explained. "It's so far away, very few *farangs* ever go there. Before getting on the ferry, you have to register with the Ministry of Tourism so that the Thai government has documentation of who has gone out there and can respond to all the letters from parents who write wanting to find out where their children are. Once a month, the local police send a fishing boat to retrieve the naked *farangs* who are living like cavemen in the jungle. Anyone who's overstayed their visa is taken to the border and released into Malaysia.

Sometimes, the travelers can't even remember their own names or what country they're from. That's when Interpol has to check fingerprints and missing person files."

I wanted to hear more, but soon the guards were shouting for the men to return inside. "Next time, bring a newspaper," he whispered.

That afternoon, I walked back from the prison with Brigid and Annemarie, two German girls who were staying in a guesthouse around the corner from me. The midday sun bore down on our shoulders, and my mouth was so dry I could have stooped to drink from the open drainage ditch if there'd been any water running through it. If we'd been smart, we would have flagged down a rickshaw, but even the drivers had nestled their bikes up against the wide trunks of the frangipani trees. The men were so thin they could easily stretch themselves out on the metal frames for a nap, their feet resting on the handle bars and heads on the leather seats.

Brigid and Annemarie told me they'd been living in Chiang Mai for nine months. When I asked them if they came to Thailand because their friend was in jail, they just laughed. "We didn't even know him before we left Hamburg," Annemarie explained.

"Nay. We knew there were Germans in prison here," Brigid added. "Some of our friends had visited them before, so we decided to give them some company. Now we cannot leave. It must be something like the way you feel when you have a baby; you are too scared to go away because you think something bad might happen when you are gone."

"What about traveling?"

Annemarie shook her head. "These are our plans now. We just go to Penang when it's time to renew the visa. It wouldn't be right to leave with him locked away like that. If it weren't for us, he'd have no one."

"Are there other Germans in there too?"

"There are three or four, and one was just sent home," Brigid told me. "It was a transfer or such. Arranged by the courts. The Thai people don't have the money to waste feeding *farangs* in jail. Their drug laws are only so strict because our countries are forcing them to be that way. Why should the Thais have to pay for our criminals? And you Americans are the worst. So much talk against drugs, but no one does anything."

"Am I the only American who visits?"

Brigid thought for a moment. "There was a girl. Younger than you, I think. Your American was very fond of her. She was always rushing about with a man on a motorbike. There was some business between her and your prisoner. Drugs, probably."

I didn't know Eric very well, and I didn't like him much, but I couldn't stand to think of him with some drug dealing American girl. Even though he was in jail, he told me he'd been set up, he was innocent, and I wanted to believe him.

When I returned to the guesthouse, I sat down in the garden and ordered a glass of sugar cane juice. The air was still and hot. Everyone had retreated to their rooms to cool off. Lying on the table in front of me was a *Bangkok Post*. I opened up the paper to a quarter-page ad.

MISSING IN THAILAND
CARA DURYEYE
LAST SEEN: BANGKOK
DISTINCTIVE FEATURES: HUMMINGBIRD TATTOO ON RIGHT SHOULDER
ONE MILLION BAHT REWARD

It was that girl again. I guess in some way, even then, I must have believed in fate because I knew there had to be a reason I kept coming across her name. I didn't care about the reward. I never would have turned her in. I just wanted to know if she was still alive and to find out what it took to survive like she did.

If I left Thailand that day, I knew I'd always wonder what would have happened if I'd stayed. How could I return to the States and pretend that nothing had changed? I'd already learned too much to ever be happy sitting in a lecture hall listening to some professor drone on about personality theory or statistical methods. Besides, I was becoming more self-sufficient. Before the trip, I relied on other people to do too many things for me, but without Ben, I started making decisions on my own. Sometimes, I joined other travelers and went sightseeing along the river or out to villages up in the hills. Other times, I was alone. Few people on the street ever bothered me. When I was with Ben, strangers saw us as an identifiable unit; a couple; a concept that crossed most cultural lines. By myself, I was an anomaly with no properties to characterize me: no boyfriend, no girlfriend, no briefcase, no babies. All predators gazed at me, then looked the other way.

I started sleeping a lot. When I slept, I didn't think about anything, or wonder why Ben left me. Each day, I stayed in bed until the sun forced its way through the wooden slats of my window and covered my face with fans of warm light. By that time of day, the air had become so thick, perspiration just sat in the hollows of my skin, forming round pools below my neck and underneath my arms. I took lots of showers, even though I knew it was useless and I'd just start sweating after I got out. Then, I'd slip on a cotton dress, tie my hair up over my neck, and tiptoe downstairs for a cup of Nescafé. Often, I'd find a copy of the latest *Bangkok Post* or *International Herald Tribune*. That was how I knew the date. As I flipped through the news, I saw that the same events from weeks before were still churning on: the bickering in the Middle East; the fighting in Rwanda; the politicians in America and Europe wrestling for power. I was aware that all that went on, but back home, I never paid much attention to it. Since leaving San Francisco, the world had become smaller, and other people's misery seemed to have more meaning to me.

I began taking long walks to parts of the city I'd never been to. If my destination was far, I rented a bike and peddled along the flat roads until I reached the outskirts of the city. The countryside seemed to calm me. Although I read about women who thrived on being alone, I wasn't one of them. Even when I was active and there were lots of people around, I still felt lonely. Always, in the back of my mind, I tried to convince myself that if I just stayed in Chiang Mai one more day, or one more week, Ben would return.

I counted out the remainder of my traveler's checks and figured that if I was careful I could stay in Thailand for another three months. That worked out well because it was roughly that long before my airplane ticket expired, and I only had to renew my visa once. To save money, I began storing bags of crackers, potato chips, and other snacks up in my room so I wouldn't have to eat at the nearby restaurants. People didn't need to eat three meals a day. It seemed so decadent, especially when there were Thais who only ate curried rice and still lived in wooden shacks without running water or electricity. If I ate at all, I bought dinner from an outdoor stand where I ordered a cheap plate of pad thai or chicken and rice. When the meal was ready, a little girl with dusty legs, dressed in a plaid school uniform and flip-flops a couple of sizes too big, would put down her homework and deliver the food, always keeping one eye on me, the hungry *farang*, until her mother shouted something in Thai that would make her scurry back to her studies.

Each night before visiting day, I'd lie in bed unable to sleep, listening to the blades of the ceiling fan cut through the thick air, waiting for the first birds to sing. By dawn, if I fell to sleep at all, I was easily awakened by the putter of early morning motor scooters as they sped through the empty streets. Then, hot and groggy, I showered, dressed, and made my way over to the river to buy the cigarettes and newspapers Eric instructed me to bring.

He began writing me. His letters usually arrived at the guesthouse just before I went to see him the next day. Some days, I didn't receive them at all, and he'd get angry when I didn't bring what he asked for. At first, he thought that someone at the guesthouse was stealing my mail and practically ordered me to move out before something worse happened. I kept telling him that I wasn't doing anything wrong, but he was convinced that the Thais were spying on me and soon I'd end up in jail like him.

Ben never wrote, not a card or a letter. A British traveler once told me he met an American named Ben up in Chiang Rai, a smaller city farther north. He didn't say anything more specific, but I knew by the way he looked at me that there were some details he was leaving out. Maybe Ben had found another girlfriend, or, more likely, was just so wasted he was no longer capable of getting off his ass and coming back.

I started counting the days until my next prison visit, and Eric began waiting for me near the gate, no longer holding back with the others. I always suspected it was the cigarettes he was waiting for and that he wouldn't want me to visit if I didn't bring the goods that he requested. Sometimes, I made plans to enter empty-handed, no newspapers, books, or imported smokes, but I never had the nerve. If he perceived the slightest infraction, I knew he'd shut me out and then I wouldn't have any reason to continue visiting him.

"I'm not some kind of goddamn criminal," he told me one day. "I shouldn't be in here. The shit wasn't even mine. They found it in my girlfriend's clothing. She was the one dealing, not me. One week I'm in paradise and the next I'm in hell."

"The Thais would say it's your karma," I joked, but he wasn't having it.

"Don't give me that karma crap. I'm from the West. I need answers. What have I done wrong?"

He was furious. I understood that. He teased me about hanging around Chiang Mai when I could have been lying on some beach in southern Thailand, and he scolded me for not making more friends, even though he gave feral looks to anyone who sat down near us. When I asked him about the American girl who Annemarie said used to visit him, he claimed he didn't know who I was talking about.

"Well, how many visitors do you have?"

"Can you imagine what it's like being stuck in here talking to the same people day after day? If there was someone new, I'd sure as hell remember."

"But why'd she visit you?"

He shrugged. "Why do you come?"

I'd been thinking about the answer to that question for several weeks and only had one real response. "Because you expect me to."

He blew cigarette smoke out the side of his mouth and started to shake his head. "You might as well stop then. If I ever had any expectations, I don't anymore. To want something in here is poison."

I sat still in that heat, wondering if I should tell him how each time I visited, I swore I was never going to come again, but when I'd get back to the guesthouse, I didn't know what I'd do if I wasn't going to see him.

"Why are you still sitting here?" he asked suddenly. "Listen to what I just said to you, and you're the only one who fucking cares. You *do* care about me and not these other assholes, right?"

When I first walked into that prison yard, it hadn't been to visit him, but then I started looking for him when the gates opened. I also thought about him late at night when the heat left me too uncomfortable to sleep. That's when I tried to picture what his cell looked like with the scores of other men lying on their mats counting the hours, days, weeks, years until they got their lives back.

"You've got to help me get out of here. I can't stay here another month," he begged.

Even though I knew that must be how all the prisoners felt, there was something about the desperation in his voice that made me think he was serious. By then, the humidity made the air so heavy, drops of sweat were slipping down the back of my neck and tickling me underneath my arms. Before he could continue, the guards began shouting for the men to get back inside. "I think I can bring a *Newsweek*," I told him, trying to act as if he'd never mentioned anything that sounded like escape.

There was an influx of tourists in town and there weren't many empty rooms available, so when Brigid and Annemarie returned from a trip into the hills, they moved into a room next to mine with an American they'd met named Jake. When I first met Jake, he frightened me. He was much older than we were and had a round face that was covered with a full black beard. His fingers were wide and swollen, as if he worked on intricate machinery all day that had left his hands irritated and bruised.

When Jake wasn't rolling a joint, it was because he was too high to do so. For whatever reason, Brigid and Annemarie never left his side. In the late morning, after most of the guests had wandered off to go sightseeing or shopping, I usually found the three of them downstairs slouched around a table, dark sunglasses shielding their bloodshot eyes.

At first, I didn't want to get high with them, but it just seemed so boring to watch them become giddy, their laughter leaving me far behind. So by the time Eric began seriously talking about escape, I guess I wasn't thinking clearly. Now, I wonder why it hadn't been enough for me to just laze around the guesthouse drinking coffee and smoking joints like everyone else. The more I thought about Eric, the more I knew that Ben had been right. I had no business with those prisoners. There wasn't anything I could ever do for them, but when visiting day came around, the urge to finish something always came over me.

Jake teased us for going.

"You are jealous," Brigid told him. "If this were a women's prison, you'd be first on line."

"You girls just like your men behind bars. Then they won't give you any trouble."

"We will return in no more than three hours," Annemarie assured him, as I hurried upstairs and tried to put together enough baht to buy the usual carton of cigarettes. That was when I realized I was down to my last fifty baht note, which wasn't nearly enough for Marlboros. If I wanted to get more money, I'd have to cash another traveler's check, but we didn't have time for that.

Most Westerners in Chiang Mai are not in a hurry, but we walked quickly along the cracked sidewalks and crumbling curbs, rushing to get on line before the gates opened. Along the way, I bought some Thai smokes and hoped they would do. Eric was going to have to get used to economizing if I was going to spend more time with him. Once, he even suggested that I move somewhere cheaper to live, but the places he recommended were Thai flophouses far away from the tourist area. Although I'd seen an occasional Westerner emerge from them, the buildings didn't look very hospitable, and besides, if Ben ever returned, he'd never be able to find me.

The line against the prison wall was shorter than usual. The French girl wasn't there, but I reminded myself that I shouldn't care. Jake had been explaining how we mustn't expect certain things to happen or rely on other people to help us out because we'd always end up disappointed. That made perfect sense.

The guards allowed us through the gates with their usual passive scrutiny, as if behind their mirrored sunglasses they were calmly waiting for us to set our own traps, which one day we'd spring on ourselves. Everyone moved slowly, so it took a while for the prisoners to be brought out. Eric was the first. As the men trickled off to their companions, I saw that the Frenchman wasn't among them. Somehow, his girlfriend must have known not to come.

Brigid and Annemarie went straight to Bernd who looked sullen and sickly. How much did he know about their friendship with Jake? Maybe he thought it was sexual. It wasn't. Jake gave the impression that he had long ago lost interest in Western women and was only turned on by Asian beauties that he paid for late at night when he slipped away from us at the bar. Sometimes, I caught him staring at me as if I reminded him of someone. When I first tried to talk to him, he seemed bothered and bored, but later I realized that this was his way of playing it safe. He had pushed me away from the start because he had no room for a person like me in his life.

During prison visits, Eric began sliding his fingers through the wire mesh. The holes had been stretched by so many desperate fingers that they were nearly large enough to squeeze an entire fist through. I wanted to pull away, but if I did I knew he'd never try again, so I let him sweep his fingertips over my skin as if they were seeding my pores with fairy dust. Looking back, I see that he was preparing me. The entire time I visited, he was sizing me up to see if I could handle the task he was about to put before me, and then when he thought I was ready, he got down to business.

On the day I rushed there with Annemarie and Brigid, Eric seemed more anxious than usual. When I pulled out the pack of Thai cigarettes, he stared at it as if I had just lifted a dead baby out of my knapsack.

"What's wrong?" I asked him.

He started shaking his head. "What kind of crap is that?"

I looked helplessly at the package dangling from my hand.

"How do you expect me to smoke that shit? And I asked for the *Herald* too. Don't tell me you didn't get my letters again?" He stopped for a moment, as if he actually expected me to answer him, but before I could explain, he was off on another rant. "Do you think it's easy living here? I've done eighteen months. I have at least four years to go. By the time I get out I'll be thirty-three. You're free now. I asked you for a few simple things, but look at you. You're too fucked up to do them."

"There's nothing wrong with me."

"I didn't just get to be like this. It took time, like fungus rotting away at wood. You don't even see it yourself, but everyone can tell you're wasted."

I sat up straight and tried to run my fingers through my hair. It was true. I hadn't been making much of an effort, but I didn't think I looked so bad either. My hair certainly wasn't a tangled mess like his, or even as messy as Brigid's. "I'm fine," I told him. "Besides, what have I done?"

He didn't seem convinced. "You're all alike. It's as if there's no one else in the world." Then he moved closer and whispered, "Prove to me that you're different. Show me you're not just some fucking selfish bitch."

I had no idea what he was talking about. Until then, I'd found him strangely comforting. Certainly, compared to where he was, my situation never seemed so bad. "I need money," he continued. "Not a little money. I mean baht, and lots of it. No fucking Thai is going to tell me how to spend the next four years of my life. Being constantly stoned and looking the way you do isn't going to help me. It's only going to start attracting people's attention."

I took a cigarette from the open pack. The whole situation reminded me of being a teenager, sitting silently at the judgment of my mother's overactive imagination. So eager was she to tackle the challenges of adolescence, I hadn't even tasted a drop of liquor when she offered me a drink, or touched a cigarette when she set aside a place in the house for me to smoke. I wasn't even having sex when she took me to get birth control.

Eric fell silent.

"Are you finished?" I asked, annoyed at his critique.

"I was finished before I ever met you. I'm begging for my fucking life. Do you know Pascal, the Frenchman? He's got pneumonia. AIDS. He's going to die. Fucking die! No one's clean in here. If I don't already have it, I'll get it soon. You have to help me. You're the only hope I've got."

I stared at the rusted wire that separated us. What did I know about the Thai legal system? Didn't he have any friends or family who could help? How had I become the only person available? As if to answer my questions, he glanced around quickly and then removed a small packet from his pocket and slid it under the grate. It was soft and squishy and fit snugly into the palm of my hand as if it'd been made just for me. I had no idea what it was, but I knew if I left it on the table, I could be accused of bringing it in. If I called attention to it and blamed Eric for giving it to me, they'd probably lock him away for ten more years.

Soon the guards were shouting for us to go. Eric stood

watching, holding two fingers before his lips. He wanted it to be our secret, so I slipped the little package into my shirt and lined up to leave.

That day, I didn't wait for Brigid or Annemarie. I'm sure they wondered why I ran off so quickly. After most visits, we usually took our time to acclimate to the world without bars. Sometimes we stopped for a lemonade or coconut water at a corner stand, but I knew I wouldn't be safe until I reached my room and could lock the door behind me. I had no idea what he had handed me. It could have been an address for a lawyer, his parents' phone number back home, or a few small jewels he wanted me to hide for safe keeping.

No one seemed to notice as I reached the guesthouse and dashed upstairs. When I unlocked my door, I saw the room was a complete mess. Dirty shirts, shorts, and dresses lay on the floor. Drying underwear hung from the bedpost. A damp towel was slung across the one wooden chair, and the whole place reeked of mildew. On the table, the book I was reading, *Patty Hearst: Her Own Story*, lay splayed beneath my diary, pens, stamps, Eric's letters, and clippings from the *Bangkok Post*. I sat down on the corner of the mattress and dipped my hand into my bra. The packet was still there, its folded corners jutting into my skin. When I opened it up, a wad of dark brown goo stuck to the plastic wrap. I didn't know for certain what it was, but I quickly crumpled up the paper and shoved it to the bottom of my knapsack, hoping that if I didn't see it, it wouldn't be there.

That evening, we all met downstairs in the café. Brigid had some sad news. She'd seen Juliette, the French girl, who told her that her friend, Pascal, had died. His body was being flown back to Belgium. "Don't they have doctors?" I asked, wondering how the Thais could let something like that happen.

Brigid shook her head. "Even if they did, why should they waste their time and money when he was just going to die anyway."

"Well, what's she going to do?"

"Maybe go back home," Brigid answered.

"No," Annemarie said. "How can she go home after this? How can anyone go home?"

Jake made some kind of noise, implying that it certainly wasn't the worst case he'd heard of. In any event, we all went over to Juliette's guesthouse to see how she was doing.

Jake walked alongside us taking long strides, slipping between parked motor scooters and bicycles as if he were a panther prowling through an urban jungle. He seemed to relish being mobile. His knapsack was one of the smallest I'd ever seen: a little green pouch fraying at the edges that never left his shoulders and always had a canteen of water dangling from its side. Once, I asked if he took the knapsack off to sleep, but he just laughed and asked, "Who sleeps?" The water seemed to represent something deeply personal for him. Even when I was thirsty, I was afraid to ask him for a drink. In the world of Jake, everyone was responsible for carrying his own water.

Slowly, I learned more about him. He was a Vietnam vet, shot down on his first tour of duty. The pilot died, but Jake and two others tried to make their way out of the jungle. After five days, they were captured and put into a prison camp. He claimed to have lost two years and fifty pounds to the North Vietnamese. When the war was over and the prisoners were exchanged, he was flown back to the States. Something must have happened, because by seventy-nine he was back in Southeast Asia.

Juliette lived at Shangri-La, a flat two-story American-style motel. In Thailand, it was very unusual to see a building so lacking in beauty. Usually the guesthouses were in old homes with small stairwells that twisted off in different directions—none of the straight lines and practical terraces found in the States—but this building seemed to symbolize the new era of Thai architecture: modern, inhospitable, and utilitarian.

We entered through a breezeway that led to a flat, well-tended lawn in the back. Perhaps the entire place had been constructed in reverse. Except for the strange entranceway, there didn't seem to be any other access from the street. On the wall of what looked to be a garage was a traditional shrine with colorful pictures of Buddha, incense, fresh flowers, and oranges that hung above more mundane objects such as rusting bicycles, gardening equipment, and a picnic table. Several Thais and three or four *farangs* were squeezed onto the picnic table and were playing Trivial Pursuit. A fat man jumped up and approached us with a wide smile. "You want room?" he asked, looking at Jake, as if the male in our group would naturally answer for us all.

Jake started to speak in Thai, but was cut off by the man's desire to sell us something.

"How about rent motorbike? We have motorbikes very cheap. Very fast. Trek to hill-tribe village? Smoke opium with the headman? I take care of everything. No worries."

Jake laughed at him, and the man's smile quickly faded as he shook his head at our disrespect and retreated to the picnic table where he inched himself back into place at the bench. The others carried on with the board game, ignoring us as we wandered into the backyard.

We didn't have to look very far. Juliette was sitting on a plastic chair on the second-floor landing. Although we hardly knew her, she seemed glad to see us, and right away started talking about the prisoner, Pascal. "I knew him for only six months or so," she explained, "but time is different here. He was in prison since eighty-nine. You saw him yourself. He was not in good health."

"Did he have any family?" Brigid asked.

"I do not know about them, and they do not know about me. I don't think they want to know. I am from Paris and they are from Belgium. We are very far apart at home."

Jake pulled out a box of matches to light the joint Juliette had rolled.

"I have no friends here," she continued. "I came with some, but they have traveled on. That was ages ago. They're probably back in France by now. Sometimes I wonder if they think what has happened to me."

Brigid took a drag off the joint and looked at Annemarie. "I'm never going home."

Juliette nodded and exhaled. "I will go back soon. Nothing means the same to me anymore. If it's no good, I can always return."

I asked her how long she'd been away, and she thought for a moment, then counted out four years. "Of course, that means I'll have to leave my job. Please don't tell Mr. Tam. He may kill me if he finds out."

None of us knew what kind of work she did, but I

didn't want to ask. In Thailand, most Westerners lived any way they wished. The Thais believed if your karma was bad, you'd pay for it in the next life, and that bit of knowledge was good enough to keep them from sneering at unacceptable behavior without judgment being cast. But Brigid wanted to know.

"I'm a dancer," Juliette told us.

"A ballet dancer?"

Juliette gave Brigid a funny look, as if she had never heard such a silly remark before. "I dance for men. I have worked all over the world."

For some reason, I couldn't picture her in a Bangkok sex bar where I'd seen Thai girls dressed in sequined bathing suits tottering on high heels and slithering up and down silver poles, waiting for men to request their numbers. Juliette seemed more high class than that, but maybe that was her attraction.

"It's not so bad, if you don't mind that kind of work," she added, pointing a well-toned calf toward the terrace railing so that her sleek muscles became taut and we could see that she'd once been properly trained.

"Do you have to have sex with them?" Annemarie asked.

"You won't make much money if you don't."

Brigid and Annemarie looked at each other, but I couldn't tell if it was because they were interested or appalled. They were funny that way. They'd been together for so long, they'd become almost like twins and could communicate without even speaking.

"I can't talk about it too much. Mr. Tam is the guesthouse owner's brother."

"Can you crash here for free?" Jake wanted to know.

"It's not as good as all that because they've got the key. If I don't show up for work, Mr. Tam can come and get me. They could beat me and nobody would say a word."

I liked Juliette. She wasn't one of those innocent travelers I met who were dreamily making their way through the cultural wonders of Southeast Asia. So, as the sun began to slip lower in the sky and flocks of crows invaded the nearby trees, the others decided to go for dinner, but I stuck around and watched as Juliette put on her makeup and got ready for work.

"If you want a job, I am sure Mr. Tam will give you one. He likes Caucasian women," she told me, reaching out and touching my hair, then making a disapproving noise. "But you really must take care of yourself. You haven't been in this country very long, have you? Your friends, the ones you came here with, what do you know about them? How do you know you can trust them?"

"I don't know much about anyone anymore."

Juliette tilted her head and started brushing out her hair. "Being alone can be a good thing, but it can also be dangerous. You must have people you can trust."

"Like Annemarie and Brigid?"

"I am not talking about anyone in particular."

"Eric?"

"Who?" she asked, turning away from the mirror where she had been applying her lipstick.

"That American in jail."

Juliette shrugged. "Pascal called him a hothead American, always making up stories."

"What kind of stories?"

She puffed out her cheeks and exhaled from between her lips. "Oh, I don't know. This or that. Stories about getting out. Escape. To Pascal, he was just another crazy, doing stupid things. Always talking big." Then she looked sad for a moment.

"Didn't Pascal want to escape too?"

"Not when I knew him. By then he was too sick to care. He used to smoke a lot of dope, you know. That was one thing that helped."

"Isn't that illegal?"

"And so." Juliette smiled. "You are a bit naive, don't you think? People in Thailand have been smoking opium for centuries."

I watched her stand up, shimmy before the mirror, and then drop to a low plié. Her arms were bent in front of her in a wide arc and her back was perfectly straight. I could tell that she'd once been a beautiful dancer. "Have you ever seen Eric with another girl?" I asked.

She thought for a moment. "There was another," she said rising to a *relevé,* as if she were warming up at the barre. "He kept saying she was going to get him out. No one thought she could help, so when the girl disappeared, everyone laughed because they were right."

"What happened?"

"Who knows? After that, I saw her around Chiang Mai for a while. I think she even came to ask Mr. Tam for a job, but of course he didn't give her one. He said she looked too much like a boy, and he doesn't like girls with tattoos."

Bending her torso low and holding her right arm out to her side, she rose again and her face flushed pink. "It was of a small bird. How do you say it, a hummingbird, very beautiful, right there on her shoulder." She picked up another joint, licked the rolling paper to secure the seal, and slid it into her handbag. "Would you like to accompany me to work?"

We strolled along the wide boulevards on our way downtown. Night had not quite fallen, and the sky was still streaked with low purple clouds. I tried to hide my excitement, but the coincidences were too many. The eyes of the girl, Cara Duryeye, still blazed in my mind from the Bangkok poster.

Soon, we turned into a narrow lane of shops that changed from tea gardens and provision stores to sex clubs and girlie bars whose window fronts were trimmed with eight-by-ten head shots of the dancers inside. The girls in the pictures looked young, no older than fifteen or sixteen, their lips smudged and cheeks darkened the way lipstick and rouge show up in poorly printed black-and-white photographs. I searched for Juliette's photo, but her face wasn't there. She must have been the treasure Mr. Tam kept hidden behind a dark curtain, secluded in a secret room inside; the kind of girl Japanese businessmen paid thousands of baht for.

"Nothing will be going on for a while, so maybe if you want to come in and Tam sees you, he'll offer you a job."

For a moment the idea sounded exciting. I imagined wearing sexy clothing, eating at expensive restaurants, and having rich foreign boyfriends, but then I remembered the life Juliette had just described: being locked away in a room where someone else held the key. I shook my head.

"You are wise and lucky to be able to make such decisions," she said kissing me on both cheeks, then ducking into the open doorway. "I will see you again, *non*?"

I waved goodbye, hoping that she was right.


Paranoia started like a sickness, creeping through and infecting my entire body. I didn't leave my room except to go downstairs to the café. I'd heard stories from other travelers about full-scale raids on guesthouses, everyone's nightmare, and kept thinking it might happen to me. The opium was still buried somewhere deep in my knapsack. It would have been so unfair if I were busted for something that wasn't even mine. Eric had never really given me a choice whether to participate in his little scheme or not.

From the garden I kept a vigil on all visitors entering and exiting the guesthouse. Whenever I saw someone looking suspicious, my heart started racing and I broke into a sweat, certain that the person was looking for me. I tried to keep Jake out of my room because I was afraid he'd find the stuff. He was a hunter, attuned to his surroundings.

There was a lot I didn't know about him. Although he was nearly twenty years older than most of the other travelers, he still seemed to hang around us faithfully. His relationship with us reminded me of the way a cat likes to bat around a mouse, without really harming it. Then when the cat gets bored and decides the game is over, he will think nothing of snapping the mouse's neck and walking away.

"Don't tell me you're one of those scribblers I see in the restaurants jotting down every goddamn bowel movement," he said one day when he saw me writing in my journal.

"It's not that kind of a diary," I told him, embarrassed that he had found out that I kept such a self-conscious hobby. I expected him to pursue it and eventually grab the notebook and read what I'd written, but he just nodded and took a seat beside me on my bed.

"I knew someone in the army who kept a diary," he admitted. "He wasn't the type you'd think of doing anything like that, but he did. It was as if he just knew something really big was about to happen to him and he wanted to capture every moment. We told him that nothing anyone wanted to read was ever going to happen, but we were assholes. When something did happen, it was too late. He was dead, and he couldn't write about it anymore. The diary was sent to his folks at home. Besides a live soldier, it was the best thing they could have gotten back from the war. The funny thing about that diary was, he never knew if what he was writing was ever going to mean anything to anyone else. For Christ's sake, this guy had written about the food he ate in the goddamn mess tent and the weather each day. He didn't write about anything heavy like what it felt like to be eighteen years old and dropped into the middle of a fucking battlefield where everyone was shooting at you and you couldn't tell who the enemy was and who was on your side. He wrote as if it were just another day: 'Today we ate green eggs and ham. Oh yeah, Joey got his head blown off by a 122 millimeter shell. His guts hung off the palm fronds like red tinsel on a Christmas tree.'"

"Hey, that's pretty good," I said, shoving my notebook beneath a few other papers so he couldn't see it.

That was the first time Jake really talked about the war. In the beginning I was curious, but I  kept quiet and didn't pester him about it. How did I know he wasn't one of those vets who went berserk at the mention of Vietnam? When we were with the others, he always seemed to be moving too fast, constantly racing from one place to another, but as he spoke about the dead soldier, he was tranquil, as if his thoughts had become trapped in some sort of stasis between memory and immediacy.

"I hated those Viet Cong gooks. What the fuck were we

fighting for? It was their country. We should have just let them go at it and kill each other. What did I care what kind of government they had?"

"I was only three years old," I reminded him.

Jake shook his head. "You girls amaze me. You come to Thailand thinking you're in some kind of fantasy. It's cheap as dirt here. You like the sun. You like the food. No one bothers you. No responsibilities. You can wear short skirts. You can fuck Thai boys. You can pretend to be on some far-out freaky holiday. But look at that French girl, Juliette. She's just a fucking sex slave."

"She can leave any time she wants."

Jake grunted. "She's worse than those prisoners who you visit in that jail, because at least at the jail they know when their time is up. With her, the Thais give her a room and all the weed she can smoke, until she's so fucked up, she couldn't leave if she wanted to."

"You heard her. She said she's going home soon."

"She's not going anywhere. You can't be free if you're beholden to anyone. I've been away since seventy-nine. No one's looking for me. I'm not anyone's sex slave. I'm MIA. Shit. Everyone forgot about me a long time ago."

Black clouds began to cover the sky, a prelude to the monsoon season. Each afternoon at around two o'clock, the clouds rolled in and released a fifteen-minute downpour that steamed up the sidewalks and flooded the avenues, actually creating more humidity than relief from the heat.

"Didn't you come to Chiang Mai with some guy?" he asked.

I nodded.

"Some people might think you're staying here for that

prisoner. If you are, you're wasting your time. There's nothing you can ever do for him."

"Maybe he needs my company."

"He's just using you. He probably thinks you'll help him escape."

"I doubt that," I told him weakly.

Jake grinned, licked two of his fingers, and extinguished the joint we were passing between us. "That's cool. I just thought you could use some help. I've tried to escape from a lot of places too, you know."

I stared at him, wondering if he would be able to help me get rid of the opium. Then the responsibility would no longer be mine alone. Maybe he knew how to sell it, or another way of dumping it without arousing suspicion. "If you were given something illegal," I began.

He grinned as though a stuck door had finally sprung open. "First thing I'd want to do is unload it. You don't want to get caught with it in your room."

I stopped talking for a moment and shook my head, thinking I was giving too much away.

"Come on Maddy. Besides, I already know. Maybe it was meant for me."

I laughed nervously, and he put out his hand. "Okay. Give it here."

"I think he wants me to sell it and then bribe some Thai official," I told him, pulling out the package.

Jake sat back and grinned, then opened his Swiss Army knife and began cutting his fingernails, flicking the slivers out between the window slats. When he was done, he licked the blade, stuck it into the sticky wad of opium, and rubbed it across his tongue. "This stuff won't buy a rat out of a hole," he spat.

"What about selling it to other *farangs*?"

"I'm not an asshole. *Farangs* are more likely to call the police. Too much democracy makes them think they've got the right to a fair drug deal."

"How much do you think it's worth?"

Jake tugged on his beard. "Not much. Maybe fifty, seventy-five dollars."

"That's never going to get him out of jail. What does he want me to do with it?"

"How about smoking it?" Jake laughed.

"You just told me it was shit."

"Shit for any serious money, but maybe it'll calm you down." He took out a small pipe from his shirt pocket and blew through the lip to clear the passageway, then cut away at the opium and scooped it into the bowl. When he lit it, the smell was harsh like burning dirt. After inhaling deeply, he offered it to me, then leaned back against the cinder block wall and closed his eyes.

I watched as he relaxed, still holding the lighter out in my direction. What harm would it do? I had no problem smoking marijuana. Maybe it *would* make me feel better. So I took the pipe and lit the bowl, sucking hard to draw in the smoke. At first I didn't feel a thing. Then after a few minutes, I felt something massive and heavy pressing down on my shoulders, forcing me to lie back onto the mattress. At the same time, I had this illusion that my body was separating from my mind and I was lying there watching my physical self split apart and float away.

We stayed slumped like that for some time, two statues blending into the concrete wall. Every once in a while, I thought I should say something, make a little conversation, let him know I was still there, but when I tried to open my mouth, my tongue seemed too heavy to ever utter a thing.

I don't know how long we stayed like that, but sometime later there was a knock at the door and we quickly moved apart. Annemarie and Brigid peered into the room. "We are thinking about going to the night market for dinner," Annemarie said.

Jake grinned lazily, glancing at me. I shook my head. I didn't feel like eating, and moving from the bed was about the last thing on my mind, but he rose and tapped the pocket where he'd slid the rest of the dope. "I'm with you," he told them as he winked at me and ushered the girls out the door.

*L*ast night I had one of those dreams. I was falling down a long tunnel and I kept on falling with nothing to stop me and no place to land.

All day I stay in my room, a water bug living in a gutter ditch. Each footstep makes my heart pound quicker. Any time someone looks at me, I know he can read my mind. I wish I could just disappear, or take back the days I spent at that prison and the moment Eric gave me that opium. Now, the only time I feel safe is at night, after I've smoked a few bowls and I'm sitting in the thick air listening to the chatter of a million different languages being carried on at once.

Everyone at Lilly's thinks they know something about me. Even Tran clucks his tongue whenever I walk by the front desk. What the hell does he want? Sometimes, in developing countries, simple maladies are left untreated, but can't that incessant clacking be stopped? The spider-like ladies who crawl around on their bony hands and knees, washing down the floors and hallways with their dirty water, always seem to be laughing at me. Once my back is turned, I know they say horrible things.

Actually, if they're really so concerned, I can tell them that I take showers at least once a day and rinse out my underwear every night. Sometimes I forget to take off my shoes when I enter a room, but that's just because I'm a dirty farang, unaccustomed to Thai habits.

Yesterday, I stayed in my room while Annemarie and Brigid went off to the prison. I wanted to go with them, but didn't know what I'd say to Eric. The truth is, Jake and I have smoked all his dope. There's none left and absolutely no way we are ever going to help get him out. I can just imagine Eric waiting for me on that prison bench, as the line of visitors enters the yard and I'm not there.

At some point after smoking the remnants of a joint, I began to pack. I had to get out of there. If I keep moving, no one will find me, and maybe I can escape; become unknown. I want to turn into someone else; someone who knows how to get by on her own and isn't always cowering in her room waiting for something awful to happen.

When Brigid and Annemarie returned, I heard them stop outside my door. They knocked, and without waiting for a reply, Brigid peeked in. I guess she must have seen my bags because she looked frightened. "But where do you go?"

"Was he there?" I wanted to know.

Annemarie shook her head. "We were just talking about that. It's so funny. It was as if someone told him you weren't coming because we didn't see him at all."

"But what is happening?" Brigid asked, pointing to my things. I didn't answer.

The more I think about it, the more I realize that Juliette is right. How do I know I can trust them? I don't know anything about them. For that matter, what do they know about me? The strongest tether we have holding us together is that we're all foreigners in someone else's country, and that just doesn't seem to be enough.

The rooms at Shangri-La were small, and the concrete walls painted gray, which kept the place cool, but didn't overwhelm me with any kind of tropical beauty. For the first couple of days, I hung around, hoping Juliette would show up. She never went home to France. She probably wasn't able to save enough money to buy the plane ticket, because, as she explained, each time a customer paid for an overpriced drink, a dance, or some sexual pleasure, Mr. Tam kept most of the money. With the rest, she bought everyday items like condoms so she wouldn't catch HIV, and various lotions and scents that took a man's stench off her body.

One night, I made my way over to the red-light district to try to find her. The evening was just beginning. Touts, hired to lure tourists into their employers' bars, were slipping through the crowds. The sexually charged foreigners weren't the gaunt low-budget hippies I was used to being surrounded by, but were genuine meaty tourists who came to Thailand on package holidays from Europe, Canada, and the United States. Most wore T-shirts with logos advertising companies like Nike, Reebok, Ralph Lauren, or Calvin Klein. Others had on matching floral ensembles whose colors made them stick out like a bowl of sweets in a drab livingroom. I watched as couples peered curiously at the nightclub windows and then quickly looked away. The real customers, groups of drunken Caucasian men, stumbled along the sidewalk trying to find the best show for the least amount of money, as if the girls could be haggled for, like buying a shirt or a watch from a vendor at the night market.

The atmosphere was exciting, but I'd felt more danger walking through the Tenderloin. How could the *farangs* take their indulgence in the sex industry seriously when their tour buses were waiting at the end of the road to pick them up at a designated hour?

When I got to Lucky Lady, an older Chinese woman greeted me. "You want to see pussy open soda bottle?" she asked, as throbbing music started up and a young girl wearing a one-piece bathing suit sauntered on stage, looking like a pissed-off teenager who'd just been sent to her room. Hanging lopsided on one of her spaghetti straps was a pin with the number 12 stamped across it so she could be easily identified by her customers and the inspectors from the Ministry of Health.

"Two pussies play pussyball?" the woman continued.

"Juliette?" I shouted over the music.

The woman puckered her lips and shrugged as if I were asking her to give away an important secret. "Fuck show? Pussy eat banana?" she countered.

I wasn't getting anywhere. Maybe she didn't even understand English. I thought about asking the girl on stage, but she seemed too preoccupied sliding the inside of her thigh up and down the chrome pole. The performer wasn't graceful or sexy the way I imagined dancers to be. The others must have hated Juliette for the talent and beauty she possessed.

When I left, the music stopped. No more customers; no need to continue the show.

Outside on the street, I bought a glass of orange juice at a stall that also sold aphrodisiac drinks with names like Hard Man and Come On. The Thai vendor looked at me, probably wondering what I was doing there. "You want girl?" he asked quietly. His rotting teeth were visible beneath a yellow light that was powered by a small generator that purred like an old cat from somewhere beneath his stall.

That question no longer surprised me. It was obvious that most Thais believed Westerners came to Thailand for only two things: sex and drugs.

"I know girl. Very young. Very fresh."

I shook my head and sucked hard at the straw, trying to finish the juice in a hurry.

"You have husband who want girl? Maybe brother?"

He was getting on my nerves, and I had the revolting idea it was his own daughter he was trying to sell me. I needed to get away from him, so I pushed my empty glass across the counter, threw down some baht, and hurried toward a traveler's bar a few blocks away.

Inside Crasy Horse, backpackers sat around looking tanned and rested, as if their worlds were full of happiness and excitement. I knew how they felt: rich, intoxicated, carefree. Sometimes, I even felt that way. The longer I remained in Thailand, the easier it was for me to tell what countries the others were from. Just by listening to the way they spoke English, I was able to pick out the Scandinavians, Italians, Israelis, Australians, and Brits. Usually, after only a few words, I guessed much of their circumstances: how long they'd been traveling, who they were with, and in which direction they were going. The tanned ones came from the south; the gaunt ones had been to poorer countries like Vietnam or Cambodia. Some were unidentifiable, though. The longer they stayed away from home, the more amalgamated they became.

I sat down at the bar with one of these amorphous types. He was dressed in purple with a flaming white beard and loops of colorful beads around his neck. His clothes made him seem European. His sarcasm made me think he was American, but his accent was too weird to classify. "How long have you been in Chiang Mai?" he asked.

Although I was certain he didn't really give a shit, I counted out the weeks and told him.

"Working?"

"I don't have papers. Besides, what could I do?"

"Teach English. A lot of *farangs* do that."

"I don't think I'd be very good at it."

"So, what do you think of the 'Land of Smiles'? Not much not to like, eh? No worries." He stabbed out his cigarette and ordered another whiskey and Coke. "I've been here twelve years. I'm in the horticulture business up in the hills. Been out there yet?"

"I've been to Wat Suan Dok."

"Yeah, around there. I've got some beautiful land."

"Are *farangs* allowed to own land?"

"If you have a Thai partner, and I've got my girl."

"She's Thai?"

"Every *farang*'s dream," he said, winking at me.

"Is she here now?" I looked around the room, but didn't see many Thai women. The ones I did notice seemed to be working the crowd and looked too young to care about making any kind of long-term investment such as buying land.

"She doesn't like to come here. It gets her down."

"She doesn't like *farangs*?"

"No. She doesn't like Thais when they're around *farangs*. What do you think this country would be like without tourists?" The image of the juice man came to mind. His choice of vocation was all about the law of supply and demand. Would he be selling his daughter if someone wasn't out there willing to pay for her?

"Hey. No worries, right?" my purple friend repeated. "Do you want to get high? I've got some great Thai stick."

I followed him into the garden where we stood under strings of colorful paper lanterns, and he lit up a joint. Other people began gathering around us, drawn by the sweet smelling smoke. Soon, he was laughing and giving advice to everyone as if he'd known them all his life. I think that's what attracted people to the ex-pat lifestyle. Suddenly, *you* become the expert and are guaranteed a captivated audience that is always changing.

When I looked up, Jake was standing a few feet away. Already, I felt he had this incredible power over me, like some strong gravitational pull. I just turned, and there he was, looking as if he'd been staring at me all night. I wanted to pretend I hadn't seen him, but it was too late. He came straight for me. "We've been looking all over for you. We thought you went back home."

"I'm fine," I said, rolling the bottom of my sandal against the gravel path.

"Well, you look strange."

"It's just me. This is the person I am now."

"Okay. I'll take your word for it. How 'bout another drink? I have five thousand baht burning a hole in my pocket. We could blow it right now if you want."

I shook my head and leaned into him as a rush came on and my vision blurred. He might not have known me very well, and I certainly didn't know him either, but in comparison to the others, I felt closer to him than anyone else.

"We could go back to my room and smoke some dope," he offered.

I didn't like the thought of returning to Lilly's Guesthouse and seeing other people I knew there.

"What about your room?" he asked.

I wasn't sure I wanted him to know where I lived either, but the prospect of getting high made me give up trying to be mysterious. So we left the bar together and strolled along the dark sidewalks where the storefronts and restaurants were shut tight, as if only crazy *farangs* stayed out so late at night. Jake kept quiet. I liked the way he didn't have to talk. Some people just rattle on and on and say nothing. When there's silence, they think it has to be filled with chatter. I'm just the opposite. I like to trust someone's companionship so completely that we don't even have to speak.

"How are Brigid and Annemarie?" I asked as we reached Shangri-La and snuck up the back stairs.

"The same. They'll never change."

"And what about Bernd?"

"Still in jail I guess," he said looking around my room. "This place isn't bad. How much do you pay?"

"One hundred-twenty baht."

"And you don't even have to strip," he laughed.

"Yeah," I said, remembering his contempt for Juliette. "I never take off my clothes."

We passed the pipe between us, and soon the world became soft and fuzzy again, the way I liked it. I sat back on the bed staring at a candle's flickering flame, and suddenly Jake's presence seemed more defined, his body etched out next to mine against the contours of the darkness.

When I was thirteen, I remember my mother telling me she thought I felt too much compassion for wounded things, like an injured sparrow or stray cat. She said it was unhealthy to be attracted to so much pain, and Jake reeked of pain. He acted as though he never expected a kind thing to happen to him for the rest of his life, and I guess I wanted to prove him wrong. But if I expected anything to happen between us that night, I was quickly set straight. When I looked at him again, his eyelids were shut. While I was dreaming of his possible seduction, he'd smoked the rest of the bowl and passed out into a sweet sleep.

The next morning I woke up and Jake was gone, but I met Juliette on the staircase as she was coming home. She was with a Thai who wore a red bandana around his head. The guy didn't seem like the type who frequented Lucky Lady. He looked more like the sort I saw dressed in Levis and a T-shirt, zipping back and forth across town on his motor scooter, ferrying pretty young *farangs* from one destination to another. At first I don't think she recognized me, but then she stopped and seemed surprised. "But what are you doing here? Do you live here now?" She asked.

"I moved in a few days ago."

"And your friends? Are they with you too?"

I shook my head and glanced at the boy who was standing against the wall. He didn't look much older than sixteen, but in Thailand, age was hard to judge. I didn't want to interrupt, so I told her I'd catch up with her later.

"Well, we'll talk soon then," she agreed as she took the boy's arm and skipped up the stairs.

Although it was late in the morning and nearly ninety degrees outside, goose bumps sprung up on my arms and legs. I wasn't feeling very well and thought it best to return to my room. A few nights before, a swarm of mosquitos had feasted on my ankles and elbows making it impossible for me to sleep. I kept scratching at the bumps until I made small gashes on my legs. The mosquitos probably carried fever, too.

Lying down, the sheets chafed my skin. To keep warm, I dumped all the clothes in my knapsack on top of the bed, then crawled underneath, submerging myself below the mounds of rumpled shirts and dresses.

Hours went by. It could've been days. When I was awake, the border between consciousness and unconsciousness was a thin sheen, fragile and transparent. It dissolved easily and left me with large gaps of time during which I knew I'd been asleep, but didn't know for how long. Sometimes I woke up and my dreams seemed so vivid I actually had the sensation that I'd been somewhere else, and I felt kind of disappointed when I realized that I was still in Thailand. Maybe it was homesickness, but I never knew that homesickness could be so physical.

One dream took place in late autumn. The sun was setting over San Francisco and a single ray of golden light spilled against the upstairs eave of an old Victorian, as if a diamond had been planted in that exact wooden joint. The jewel refracted the yellow light, and I bathed in its warm glow.

In another dream, I was walking along a windswept beach looking out at seals curled up on a big rock that stuck out of the rough Pacific, like oily black dots rising above the water's surface. Ben was there and trudged ahead of me in the sand while wind slapped my face and sea spray stung my cheeks. I called out for him to wait, but when I yelled, the breeze took my voice and he never heard me.

I wouldn't say I enjoyed being so feverish, but it took

my mind off everything else. The only thing I worried about was getting better. Everyday, while lying inert in bed, I listened to the footsteps shuffling back and forth along the terrace. Certain kinds of noises told me when a group of travelers moved in or out, when the young boy swept the stairwell, or when the women came to collect the dirty sheets and towels. Then one day, the footsteps stopped outside my door and someone knocked.

"*Bon dieu,*" Juliette cried when she saw me. "What is wrong with you?"

"I think I have some kind of flu," I told her weakly.

"You look really ill."

"I haven't been able to get out of bed. I just sleep and sleep."

"Have you taken any medicine?"

"I thought it would go away."

"You should really visit a doctor. I only know Mr. Tam's doctors who treat sex diseases, but I will ask downstairs. I'm sure there's a correct doctor on this street."

I thought about a doctor and all the questions he might ask, questions I had no answers for, like how many days had I been ill or what was I doing just before I got sick? "I think I'm getting better," I told her hopefully.

"Good," Juliette smiled, "because there's someone asking for you. You know him, am I right? He came by this morning and left this note."

I grabbed the paper thinking Ben had finally written me. She must have sensed I wanted to be alone because she stood up, explaining that there was something she had to do.

The moment she was gone, I ripped open the envelope. Inside, the handwriting was unfamiliar, filled with jagged loops and scribbles. It said:

*M: looked for you at Shangri-La. No one's heard of you. Going north this morning. Meet me in Fang. Jake.*

I dropped the note on the bedside table and sunk back underneath the sheets. Ben was never coming back. He just left me in Chiang Mai, as if he were leaving an old blown out tire on the side of the road. Waiting for him was a waste of time. Maybe my sickness was a sign; my body telling me to get out of Chiang Mai. Nothing was left for me there, and I was just putting off moving forward, traveling like we'd planned. Suddenly, going somewhere new seemed like a great idea.

W*here the hell is Jake? It's been two days. I'm beginning to think I just make people disappear.
Maybe he's playing some kind of joke. I don't like
it, and it's getting kind of difficult to ignore the two guys next
door. We're the only guests here. We speak the same fucking
language! Why won't they talk to me? I'm not invisible. I don't
care what the hell they're up to. So what if they're dealing
drugs? Who isn't? Maybe only me.*

I don't remember getting to Fang. The mountain curves
made me so nauseous that it didn't matter where the bus
finally stopped, I was getting off. The town sat on a high
plateau; old provision shops and fruit stands lined both
sides of the one paved road, clutching to the only lifeline
that ran through the area. The place reminded me of an old
ghost town up in the high plains of New Mexico. Even the
guesthouse was the typical single-story motel you could
find along a state highway in the Southwest. Each of the
doors had once been painted green, but the paint had faded
over the years and the doors were now splintered and gray.
When I first saw the building, I half expected Anthony
Perkins to come striding out of the reception office, but a
squat Chinese woman in sweat pants and T-shirt greeted
me instead. The *samlor* driver, who left me at the gate,
motioned for me to go on into the compound.

"You want room?" the woman asked. "Very cheap. Air-conditioning free. TV included." When she opened her mouth, a cascade of betel nut juice fell from her lips.

I nodded, still unsure if this was the town I wanted to be in. Jake had clearly written Fang, but there didn't seem to be any guests around. Not a single bicycle or car was parked in the courtyard, and most of the motel's windows and doors had been covered with plywood.

"Come. Come," the woman insisted as she whisked the *samlor* driver away. "Very quiet here. No problem. You see."

She led me to the room closest to her office, and with several quick flourishes, switched on the lights, air conditioner, and TV, making enthusiastic noises at each surge of electricity. I tried to appear impressed even though the air conditioner spewed black smoke and the TV projected blurry images back-lit in a scarlet hue. I decided to take the room anyway, at least overnight. I didn't really have another choice. I was too exhausted to catch a bus back to Chiang Mai, even if there'd been one leaving town that day.

The old lady tried to chat, but quickly gave up when she saw how tired I was. Before she left, she lay down the rules: drinks were on sale from the rusting refrigerator just outside her office door, and no food was allowed in the room, although she claimed to be more than happy to make me dinner for a small fee. The sheets were changed every other day, and if I wanted new towels, I had to exchange the ones I had each morning.

My new room resembled the inside of a green pepper with "color" television that broadcasted images obscured in bloody red hues. (I think I watched *Kojak* dubbed into Thai, but because of the bad reception, it could have been some science fiction drama about a bald red space alien who solved crimes.) It must have been years since anyone actually slept there. The mattress was soft and lumpy; the green rug thin and worn. A quick glance into the bathroom revealed a light green Western-style toilet, matching sink, and a narrow rusting shower stall. Two folded green towels hung on the rack as stiff as washboards.

After Mrs. Chang left, I peeked out between the Venetian blinds into the lane behind the hotel. Why would anyone actually end up here, I wondered. The *samlor* driver probably received some sort of kickback from Mrs. Chang. Maybe that was how she lured her customers in. That, and the fact that there didn't seem to be another guesthouse in town. Not that there was any need for one, either.

Soon, the air-conditioning made the room too cold and I had to stand on a chair to turn the machine off. After a sputter, the gushes of air stopped in a way that made me wonder if I'd ever be able to turn the thing back on. Really, I preferred the faithful rotations of an old ceiling fan. Back in Bangkok, Ben and I had spent long hours lying on our bed, waiting for the fan's gentle breeze to send waves of cool air over our hot bodies. The rhythmic clacking of the blades always lulled us to sleep.

Later that evening, I learned that Mrs. Chang's wasn't as deserted as it seemed. I heard the rumble of motorbikes, but instead of going past the motel, the noises became louder as the drivers turned into the entranceway and pulled up in a cloud of dust. From my window, I watched two sunburned *farangs* get off their bikes and slap at the dirt covering their jeans. Together they laughed and spoke loudly in English until one of them noticed me. I was listening to my Walkman and pretended not to hear them, but I could tell by their expressions that they weren't exactly happy to see me. As quickly as they saw me, their voices died, and they nodded some unenthusiastic greeting, slipping behind the door of one of the other rooms. Typical behavior, I thought. Ben always said that Americans had an overly defined sense of privacy.

Then, Mrs. Chang, betel juice dribbling from the corners of her mouth, kindly delivered a meal of sliced beef, Chinese cabbage, and rice, quickly assuring me that she would put the charge on my bill. I never doubted that. As if the dinner also came with an unspoken invitation to watch me eat, she sat down and nodded approvingly every time I shoveled a spoonful of rice into my mouth.

"You travel alone?" she inquired, her eyes glancing sideways to my belongings, probably trying to assess who I was.

When I nodded, she clucked her tongue disapprovingly. "It's dangerous, no?"

I shrugged, and put the same question to her. After all, it was her country. If it was dangerous, she would surely know.

"For some. But pretty girl like you, why you travel alone? Why you no have husband or boyfriend to take care of you?"

"I'm meeting someone," I told her.

She looked mistrustful. "What someone you meet here?"

I smiled, wondering what kind of situation she imagined I'd gotten myself into. Then I remembered that I had, in fact, gotten into a situation that might have seemed unusual to most people. After I finished eating, I handed her the empty plate, wondering how many baht she was going to charge, and hoping she'd take the opportunity to leave, but instead, like a hen settling in on her eggs, she made herself more comfortable.

"You like Thailand, yes? You go south? South very dangerous. Must be careful. Some Thais no good. Americans good. We have Americans here right now. They my guests for many years. Sometime they go away, but they always come back. They say, 'Mrs. Chang, no problem, we be back soon.'"

"Are they the ones on the dirt bikes?"

"You like motorbike? You want to rent one? I tell them to take you for ride. You like that?"

From the room next door, I heard the screen door slam, the motorbikes start up, and I knew I'd lost my chance of going for a ride, at least for the night.

The next day, one of the men finally spoke to me. His name was Mike. He was short and stocky with stringy blond hair. Definitely not my type. His triceps bulged from his sleeveless sweatshirt and his pink skin looked as if it had just been scrubbed by steel wool.

"Game over," he announced, gazing at me as if I were some strange weed that had suddenly sprung up between the cracks in the pavement. "Why don't you just tell me what the hell you're doing up here? Are you traveling alone?"

"Why is that such a popular question?" I laughed.

"Not many *farangs* wind up here. I should know. We've been here for seven years."

"Yeah. I've seen you around," I nodded, wanting to

seem unimpressed. I'd begun to notice that with other travelers, there was some kind of agreement of eminent domain where the person living in the hotel or guesthouse the longest commanded the most respect.

"You might as well come in and meet Pete." He motioned toward the room next door.

Inside, the room reeked of body odor, mildew, and cigarettes. There was so much smoke, I could barely make out the other man lounging on the bed. "This is Maddy," Mike introduced.

"Where're you coming from?" Pete asked, in what sounded like a southern drawl. Behind him, tacked on the cinder block wall, hung an American flag.

"Chiang Mai."

He smiled as if I'd just cracked an amusing joke. "How long were you there?"

"Over a month."

"Most people get out after a week or two. Didn't some enterprising Thai try to hustle you off to a hill-tribe village?"

"I'm not into that."

"Not into smoking opium?" Mike asked.

I smiled. "I didn't say that."

I was the first guest they'd seen in months. We passed around a joint, and the room became more obscured by smoke. I could barely see Mike next to me, but I liked it that way because I didn't know what to make of him. If I was back in the States, I suppose I could have bumped into guys like them at some roadside bar up in the Sierra foothills. They were definitely not college types, or the drugged-out hippies tripping through the streets of the Haight.

They seemed to be sizing me up, too.

"Is that flag for real?" I asked.

Pete turned around and looked at the wall. "One hundred percent."

"Are you guys patriots or something?"

"It was left here," Mike explained. "This place was used for R & R during the war."

The joint he passed over was so tightly rolled, it was almost impossible to inhale. With each long drag, the men leaned back to enjoy the rush, while I waited, praying that I had the strength to get out before too long. Soon, they seemed to forget that I was there and began discussing details of some deal that was in the works.

"Do you need a fucking Thai dictionary?" Mike asked Pete. "Tomorrow means a week from tomorrow in Thai."

"When do we have to know," Pete wondered.

"Their tickets are booked for next Saturday."

"They know the routine. Joey goes on duty at five a.m. at JFK."

I got up and stretched. "I guess I should be going."

Mike jumped up and held the screen door open. "Come over any time. Beers are always on the house."

"Sure," I said, thinking they had purposely meant to frighten me.


Each evening, just as the sky became dark, Mrs. Chang made dinner. Usually, around eight, I'd stroll over to the office and sit down with her at an old card table that she set up outside her door. There was no Mr. Chang, so she was always happy to see me. I loved her duck and lemongrass soup. The broth tasted both sweet and tangy. It was especially good after walking along the hot roads all day.

By that time, my clothes hung limply around my waist, as if my body was a tent pole and the garments untethered nylon. It was not that I didn't eat. The food went straight through me. I was lucky to have Mrs. Chang there to brew up hot tea or Milo when I needed something soothing to drink. Sometimes, I thought if I concentrated hard enough, I could get rid of whatever sickness was lingering inside me.

"Maddy," she began one day, "you go into American boys' rooms. How rooms look? They okay? They clean? You can tell truth to me."

"How long have they been here?"

"Six or seven years. They my only real guests. They keep Krappy Guesthouse in business. Otherwise, who would stay here? Why Maddy, no more *farangs* come to Fang?"

I nearly burst out laughing. "What's the name of this place?"

"Krappy Guesthouse." Mrs. Chang nodded proudly. "But I not living here my whole life. Originally, I from China. Many Chinese come to Thailand. Chairman Mao no want us. When Communists take over, my family cross border and make good business here. Later come the war and American GIs flood to Thailand. Not here at first, but Bangkok. Thailand sell them girls and drugs. I have son-in-law. He American GI. He and daughter live in Texas now, but before war over, he stay in Thailand and live in jungle. Better than getting shot by other Americans. Now they have three kids and send money to me. They want I come and live with them, but I not ready." She motioned to the compound. "You should have seen. Twenty-five years ago, this place filled with GIs. Oh boy, they love to have good time. Lots of drinking, singing. Girls! Every bar filled with girls. Families send girls from all over Thailand. They make lots of American dollars. Then war over. Mr. Chang die. Seow Lin move to Texas to be with GI boyfriend. The world turn and I still here."

"Are you ever going to go to the States?"

"Sure, sure. I want. My whole family there. U.S.A. number one, but nothing wrong with living in number two country for a while. You be good girl and stay away from drugs. Don't trust no man. Then you be happy."

When Jake finally arrived, I was lying on my bed listening to the different ways the birds called to each other. First, there were two chirps and a peep from some-where off in the trees, then a peep and a chirp. The exchange continued until one of the birds just stopped. The other called out a few fruitless times but then gave up, and flew off somewhere else where he got a better response, I guess.

At first, I didn't recognize Jake. I just saw this shape against the screen door, but he came striding towards me; a giant creature coming in from the wild.

"Where've you been? I've been waiting here for days," I explained.

"Didn't anyone tell you? I had to go up into the hills."

"Who should I have asked?"

He looked at me strangely and motioned towards the rooms next door. "You've met the others, haven't you?"

"How should I have known they were with you?"

"You could have asked them."

"I was here two days before Mike even said hello."

"Well, they don't trust anyone."

"I was really sick, you know."

He nodded. "I thought maybe you went—"

"Home?" I finished for him.

"Yeah," he grinned, sitting down on the edge of my bed.

"Well, it's funny. I never really thought I'd get to be like this, and I guess there's a lot of reasons why I should've packed up by now, but whenever I try to imagine myself getting on a plane and leaving, my mind just stops. I can't see going anywhere after coming all this way. Does that make sense? I can't believe you actually live here."

"Shit. By now if I were back in the States, someone like me would be married, divorced, and working to pay child support. At least I'm not going to end up like that."

I watched as he lit a joint and inhaled deeply. Smoke billowed from his mouth and began to fill the room. I hoped that Mrs. Chang wouldn't smell it, and as if reading my mind, he got up and closed the door.

I was sitting with my back against the wall, and he lay down on the pillow below me, resting his head next to my hip. We talked some more, but I can't remember about what. It just seemed natural to start running my hand through his hair. It was thick and curly, flecked with wiry bits of gray. At first I didn't think much about it. I just wanted to make him feel good, and each time my fingers came to the end of a strand, he let out a little moan, as if it were painful to feel my touch leaving his head.

When I write about it now, I see how random it all was. Perhaps it didn't happen like that. Maybe there were signs before that I don't remember. I'm not surprised at what happened next, but I recall thinking that he hadn't been with a woman in a long time. I didn't ask. Besides, there didn't seem to be room for women in whatever operation they were running up there.

Okay. We made love. I don't like to put much meaning into that physical act, but it was quick and easy. When it was over, we looked at each other, two acquaintances surprised at seeing something familiar in each other for the first time. But then he pulled away and glanced at the door, probably wondering which one of his buddies was going to barge in first. I was worried too. I didn't want to be caught naked or considered their communal whore.

Jake sat up and relit the joint, putting the burning end in his mouth and drawing me toward him. Smoke shot out between his lips into mine. Then he leaned back and laughed.

"How much longer do you think we can stay like this before someone finds us?" I asked.

"A million years would be nice," he sighed. "How 'bout a cold beer?"

"If we go out there together, Mrs. Chang will think something's up. I can't believe how nosy she is."

"You be the point man. Once you get out there, you'll be on friendly ground."

I slipped on my sarong and folded it just below my armpits. Outside, the temperature was so high even the birds had stopped singing. Usually, the heat prevented anyone from venturing out until evening, and I imagined Mrs. Chang in her little room, dressed in her silk pajamas, splayed out on her bed underneath the ceiling fan.

I almost made it to the refrigerator when, as if on cue, she popped her head out of her screen door. "Beer at lunchtime will help you sleep good," she said grinning. "You need to rest in this heat."

I tried smiling back, but already I felt as if she'd caught me doing something I wasn't supposed to do. The weed made my tongue heavy. Even if I had been thinking clearly, I doubt I would have had the inspiration to say a word. Instead, I concentrated on taking out two Singhas from the refrigerator.

"You want some taro cake too? I make fresh. Good with coffee, you know."

I shook my head.

"You have something better to do, eh?" She nodded towards the line of rooms.

I laughed at her, as if she'd just said something incredibly stupid. Then I hurried back down the walkway, the brown bottles clinking together as I skipped barefoot along the hot cement.

I loved those first days in Fang. Usually, I woke up early, leaving Jake still sleeping at my side, and took long walks along the dirt road behind the hotel. That was when I met the real residents of Fang: men who went off into the forest with machetes dangling from their hips; women shuffling into town toward the market; and children playing games in the road with sticks and pebbles. At that hour, a damp mist still hung like a thin canopy between the branches of the trees. The dry soil crunched pleasantly beneath my feet. On either side of the road were small wooden houses resting high on stilts. Some had roofs made of tin, others were covered with layers of palm fronds.

Behind the houses was the forest, dense and green. The clean air mixed with the smell of early morning fires, and I completely forgot about the choking pollution in the cities.

The countryside around Fang was fantastic. It was hot, but not when I was riding on the back of Jake's motorbike. Together, we buzzed through town, then scrambled up into the mountains, visiting crumbling shrines and temples deep inside the jungle. Afterward, we swam beneath waterfalls and ate at small roadside restaurants. Everyone we met was friendly, and it felt great to be with Jake and realize that others were happy for us.

Some days, he took me to a waterfall not too far off a dirt road where we stayed hidden beneath the leaves, talking and dipping our feet into the water pools. Often, Thai women from a nearby village arrived with buckets hanging off their shoulders, their brown bodies wrapped in colorful batik sarongs. When we saw them come toward the water, we ducked farther into the shrubs and watched as they waded waist deep into the pond. Some slipped their buckets into the water, then poured the water over their heads, lathering themselves with a bar of soap that they passed between them. They'd chatter from the moment they arrived until they were clean and had filled their pails and left again. I was captivated by their beauty and the skill it took to bathe without jeopardizing their modesty. If they knew we were watching, they would have collapsed in shame.

One day, they brought along a girl, probably no older than fifteen. She didn't wear any of the traditional garments the older women had on. Even though the temperature was about ninety-five degrees, the girl was dressed in tight blue jeans, a fitted T-shirt, and a denim jacket. Her lips were coated with glossy red lipstick, and her hair was tied high up on her head in a long ponytail.

She followed the ladies to the water, but stood on the shore as they bathed. The women didn't talk as much as they usually did. They seemed to be listening carefully as the girl told her story. I couldn't understand what she was saying, but Jake translated for me.

"She's listing all the things her boyfriend buys for her," he whispered. "She says she has a cell phone, a hair dryer, a TV, and VCR. She wants a CD Walkman, but the others don't know what she's talking about, and now she's explaining it to them."

I was sweating because we'd been hiding in the bushes for some time, and I could feel Jake's breath on my neck, quick and light, like a reptile keeping still in the hot sun. At the watering hole, the ladies' laughter turned to concern. They continued to listen to the girl, as she started to say something that made them shake their heads and cluck their tongues. When I looked over, the girl was standing before them, holding her shirt up above her navel, pointing to a neat scar that cut diagonally across her stomach.

"She's owned," Jake told me. "That scar means she's marked."

The women came out of the water and took a closer look at the cut. The girl didn't seem to mind. She stood proudly as they ran their fingers along the line of dimpled skin.

After that, the ladies filled up their buckets as usual and walked back along the path. We slipped out of the bushes, and tears came to my eyes. I couldn't help it. Even though I knew I was different from that girl, I suddenly felt connected to her by that scar. It was visible, and whatever wound I had was not, but I felt just as incapable of protecting myself and controlling my own destiny as she was.

"Don't let them get to you," Jake tried comforting me.

"But she's so young. How could anyone do that to her?"

"I've seen younger. Prostitution is the best way for them to make money. Didn't you see the difference between her and the other aunties? I bet she can't stand coming up here to visit and living like a country bumpkin now that she's gotten a taste of the city."

"They stared at the scar as if she were showing them an engagement ring."

Jake laughed. "Hell. It's like an engagement ring. It means she'll be taken care of for the rest of her life."

"How could she let someone mutilate her like that?"

"You're lucky," he told me. "You're here by choice. Others don't have that much freedom."

I wiped my face and felt the sweat and tears mixed with dirt scratch my skin. I didn't mean to be such a baby. It was just so sad; no one was ever going to help that girl. She was doomed to spend the rest of her years living in Thailand's underworld and could never appreciate the purity of her old life again. I also knew that Jake was right. I couldn't be the judge of whether that was good or bad. I wasn't living under the same conditions and didn't have to think about survival in the same way.

Later, we stopped for lunch at a restaurant along the banks of the river. I felt shaken, as if I'd been in some kind of accident that wasn't physical, but had left me wounded in some other way. The place was empty except for a yellow-eyed myna sitting in a cage. Off to the side, our waitress was asleep, her legs propped up against a wooden chair that she'd set out in front of her. We sat down at a table on the veranda and looked out onto the murky water. Jake's face was raw from the sun, and I knew that mine probably looked the same too. The myna let out a caw every few minutes, but it was obvious that the woman wasn't about to wake up.

We stared at the slow-moving water for some time. Then Jake started to say something he must have been thinking about before we even got there. "Are you sure you're ready to be up here?" he asked quietly, as if he already knew this question was going to upset me.

"I'm here right now."

"I know, but if anything were to happen—"

"I love it here. I don't want to leave," I told him, tapping my fingers against one of the hollow bamboo poles forming a crosshatched fence that enclosed the patio. "Why? Do you think I should go?"

He rubbed his big hand across his face. "I'm not telling you what to do. You've got to make that decision for yourself."

"I *have* made a decision. I'm thinking right now, and this is what I'm thinking: Who the hell are you to tell me what to do? You're the one who asked me to come up here in the first place."

Jake nodded. "I admit, I asked you, but I probably wasn't thinking long term."

A burning feeling seared through my insides. "A couple of weeks isn't long term."

"Up here it is."

"Okay. What if I decide you're right? I pack my bags and I leave tomorrow. How would you feel then?"

He shrugged. "It doesn't matter how *I'd* feel. You shouldn't waste your time on me."

I didn't say anything more. My head was throbbing from the heat. Soon, the waitress began to stir. She saw that we were sitting at the table and quickly came over to find out what we wanted to eat. First, we ordered a large bottle of beer, and the drink seemed to do us good. When the food arrived, we began talking again. A short time later, we called for more beer and got so drunk we had to lie down on the bank of the river until we sobered up and Jake could drive home.

I spent a lot of time trying to understand what kind of business they were in. They talked about different places: the fields; the plant; and Chinese gangsters they seemed to be afraid of. But none of that really crept into my life until one morning when I bumped into Mike just before he was leaving for Chiang Mai. His hair was combed into a neat ponytail and he'd put on a clean T-shirt and jeans.

"How do I look?" he asked when he saw me.

Except for the tinted sunglasses, I hardly recognized him. "Weird," I told him.

"That's not exactly what I'm aiming for."

"Well, what do you want to look like?"

"Like king fucking *farang*," he said grinning.

I examined him up and down. He was wearing a faded YMCA T-shirt; his jeans hung loosely off his hips; and his skin was dry and red. "You look like an American who's been slow cooking for years."

"Maybe you can drift through the crowd easier than I can."

I laughed. "Drifting is my speciality."

"Fucking terrific," he said, mounting his bike. "Next time, you can go down to the city."

Since I didn't know what he was talking about, I didn't exactly refuse.

After Mike took off, I went back into Jake's room. He was sitting in an armchair reading an old *Time* magazine and listening to a Bob Marley tape. From the photograph of Mikhail Gorbachev on the magazine cover, I could tell it had been around for a few years. So far away from it all, nothing mattered to us. Historical events could have happened centuries ago, or just the other day. My own past was being wiped away too. By then, I only had the present.

"Mike just went to Chiang Mai," I reported.

Jake seemed unimpressed. "Someone has to."

"Well, what'll he do there?"

"Business."

I looked at him closely. "What kind of business?"

Jake gave me one of his looks that told me I should back off. He shifted in his seat so it became uncomfortable for me to remain on his lap where I was sitting. Then he said something I'll never forget. "Now, I'm going to give you some advice. If I were you, I'd stay as far away from us as possible, unless you want to end up being given free room and board courtesy of the Thai government."

"I'm not stupid," I argued. "I just want to know what's really going on."

"Shit! Can't you forget about it?"

"I just feel so insignificant. Like some piece of dust floating around up here, blowing one way, then another. Nobody really cares if I'm here or not."

"We have a million-dollar operation going on. We can't fuck up, or the next asshole you visit in prison might be me, and that won't be for no four or five years. They execute people for what we're doing here."

"Well, what *are* you doing?"

He lit a cigarette and blew the smoke out from the side of his mouth. "Haven't you heard a thing I've said? Getting mixed up with us can kill you, if you're lucky."

"Why'd you ever tell me about this place if you didn't want me to be here?"

"Hell, I don't know. I'm an asshole, I guess. I was lonely."

When I looked at him again, it was easy to see how much older he was than me. The pores on his face were open and large. Small lines fanned out from the corners of his eyes. It made me sad to realize how unhappy he was, as if suddenly he knew there was something between us that could never be overcome. I slung my arms around his neck. "I don't want to be anywhere else. Fang seems just right."

He became silent and pulled me closer. We kissed for a while, but it didn't feel the same. Then he stopped and moved away. "If I were you, I'd take the next bus back to Bangkok, hop a plane at Don Muang, and get the hell out of here. If you stay, you're going to end up just like us. You'll have nothing. No home, no family. It'll be as if you can't even remember where you came from."

I looked at him, but I was so close, his face seemed out of focus. I couldn't believe what he was saying. Then he started rambling on about a village in Vietnam. "In the war, I was stationed near the Cambodian border. I became friends with a young Viet guy who'd been sent to the village to be the teacher there. He was smart and could speak a little English. One day he asked me and a buddy to come into the classroom to help teach the kids English. God knows why he wanted those kids to learn the language of the fuckers who were destroying their country, but my platoon wasn't doing anything, so every day, we'd go into the hooch that was the school to be with the children. I got to love those kids. In the middle of all that chaos, they seemed happy, as if they knew nothing about the war around them. At night, I took my weapon and patrolled outside of the village, but we were lucky. There was never any action. We were just dumb grunts. To us, it felt like we were on some kind of rugged survival trip, only with machine guns, hand grenades, and surface-to-air missiles. Then one day we got orders to move farther north into the mountains. No one wanted to go. We all thought we'd have bad luck if we moved. But again we didn't see any action. We were up in those hills for three days, and when we came back down, I thought everything would be the same again: the same smiling faces, the same dusty kids running wherever the hell they pleased; the usual village routine. But before we even got close to the village, our tracking dogs froze in their paths and went down into a low crouch. They must have sensed the destruction because no matter what we did, they wouldn't go any farther. Once the men saw the dogs act that way, they became spooked too. No one would budge. Instead, we circled around the village, avoiding the worn path, and creeped through the under-brush. When I got up the courage, I looked through the thicket. The place had been demolished. No one was there: not a single mother, or child, hut, or well; nothing except a leveled area in the forest where there used to be homes. Those people could have been my enemy, but I cried for them. They weren't Commie gooks. They were human beings. I knew their names. That's when things really began to get bad."

"So you're never going to care about anything again?"

He shook his head. "You're too good for this. Look at you. You're still young, still pure."

"What about Mrs. Chang?"

"She knows exactly what we're doing here. She takes our money. No questions asked."

"I could leave right now," I offered. I was angry that his own twisted emotions were affecting our relationship, and I thought that if I got my bags packed I could catch the afternoon bus for Chiang Mai. I knew the bus schedule because each day I heard its gears grinding as it lumbered out of town.

But I was stupid. I didn't leave. Instead, I started spending more and more of my days in the jungle. The forest was serene; a place where I could be alone and think. As I walked along into the hills, I made friends with a few of the children who played in the dirt alongside the road. The first time, I smiled at them as I went by. There were two brothers and a sister. The girl looked about ten and wore a tartan dress that hung off her bony shoulders. The older boy was about eight and usually had on a school uniform, light blue button down shirt and dark blue shorts. The youngest was about one. He wore his brother's old T-shirt, which fell below his knees. Underneath he was naked, and from time to time I'd catch sight of his dusty bottom waddling back and forth as he scurried away from me.

Every day I walked by them, and they got used to seeing me. At first they were shy and usually scampered behind a tree to wait until I passed, but they must have been curious about me too, because soon they started following me down the curving dirt path that led deep into the jungle. I'd hear them jostling through the leaves, but when I looked behind, they crouched down where they were, and pretended they were examining something in the soil.

One day I led them deep into the jungle to my favorite spot: a small shrine built in the middle of a grotto that had been overrun with brush. A twenty foot reclining Buddha lay in complete disrepair, buried beneath the leaves and twigs. I probably never would have found that place, except for the statue's spiraling stone headdress that stuck out above all the jungle debris. For a while, I thought I had discovered an ancient relic that had been forgotten many years ago, until one time I noticed that the stonework had been swept clean and a garland of fresh flowers hung around the Buddha's neck. Someone else knew about the enchanted place, and whoever it was had come there to clean it.

Usually, I sat on a rock just above the Buddha's head and listened to the buzzing. I never really noticed how loud the jungle was until I heard the flies and other insects making variously pitched whirring noises as they flew past my ear. Lizards and snakes rustled in the leaves, slithering from log to log, and there were also the whoops and screams of jungle birds and monkeys hiding in the canopy above.

The overhead growth kept the hot air from infiltrating the space between the ground covering and the treetops, so I felt as if I had a private little ventilated chamber protected from the humid air outside. Sometimes, I went there with a book or to write in my journal, but once the kids started following me, I didn't need anything else to keep me entertained. The children did nothing spectacular, and we barely communicated, but they were nimble and loved to race around the broken branches and vines, looking in my direction every time they jumped off an especially high limb or balanced on a tree trunk.

I started speaking to them in my awful Thai. They had no idea what I was trying to say, but they smiled anyway. For all I knew, they didn't even speak Thai, but used some hill-tribe dialect. Soon, they figured out just when I would come by their house everyday and would catch up with me right after I passed. Once we left the dirt road and moved into the bush, the kids sped up and dashed in front of me. Sometimes, I ran along with them, until I became too hot and breathless to keep going. The girl's name was very long and she giggled before she ever got to the end of it. She called herself Nark, which seemed quite normal to her. The older boy was a mixture of rough and sweet. Each day, before we started our trek, he broke a twig from a tree and swung it around, jabbing it through the air like a sword, but then he'd surprise me and use the tip to gently tickle his baby brother under the chin.

What I liked best about the little one was the way he was being toilet trained. Living in the jungle, the kids were able to run around until they learned where to relieve themselves, usually some latrine dug outside in the back of the house. This child was in a stage between knowing he had to go and controlling where he went, so whenever the urge came over him, he just lifted the ends of his T-shirt and squatted where he was.

When I told Jake about the village kids, he warned me not to get too close to them. "You could be poisoning them. You know what they say about handling cubs in the wild. Once they get used to you, they'll trust all *farangs*."

"But I'm not hurting them."

"No, but they may come to expect things."

I stopped myself before I said anymore. By then, he'd told me stories about how the kids in Vietnam were so innocent, how they trusted American GI's because the grunts played soccer with them and gave them chocolates and chewing gum, but there were other soldiers who blew the children away for target practice.

One night, we went into town and I found a vendor outside a restaurant who sold tiny boxes of M&M's. I hadn't seen M&M's for a long time and just figured some cunning Thai had brought a shipment north, just like Jake and his buddies were transporting drugs south. Even though the candies were outrageously expensive, I bought a few boxes and kept them in my bag for the children. I wanted to watch them marvel at the bright colors before popping the round chocolates into their mouths.

The next morning, I packed up a few books, my diary, water, and the candies, and left Mrs. Chang's at the usual hour to go into the jungle. But when I passed the children's raised house, I didn't hear their laughter. I turned around and walked by again, but still saw no sign of them. Since the door to the hut was never shut, I climbed up a few rungs on a wooden ladder and peered inside. The single room was dark and had a bamboo floor. Some sleeping mats were rolled up and tucked into a corner. I didn't like the feeling that I was spying on them, so I quickly stepped down and started walking again. When I got a little distance away, I looked back and noticed a woman washing clothes at a well behind the house. I'd never seen her there before, but maybe I'd just never looked. Of course, she was the children's mother. She smiled shyly, as if she understood I was looking for them, but there was something else in her eyes that told me she'd hid them from me.

When I returned to the guesthouse, Mike was sitting outside my door smoking a cigarette. I could tell by the way he was looking at me that something had happened. "Where's Jake?" I asked.

He nodded toward Jake's room where I heard the spray of water rush from a tap.

"When did you first come to Thailand?" Mike asked.

"Sometime in early January, I think."

He looked at the date on his watch. "Do you know what month it is?"

I took a guess. "March, maybe April?"

Mike looked concerned. "You'd better find out. If it's been three months, your visa could have expired."

I always figured that when the time came to renew my visa, I'd go to Malaysia like many other travelers did, but since arriving in Fang, I hadn't exactly been concentrating on practical things.

"If you leave Thailand and ever want to come back, you should do things by the book," he advised.

"It just seems so useless. Malaysia's such a long way away."

Mike looked concerned. Then he sighed as if he were about to say something he really didn't want to bring up. "Jake wants me to let you know that he's totally against this, but if you decide to go south, there's something you could do for us. It would really help us out, and you'd be great at it too. A new face is a guaranteed delivery."

"What are you talking about?"

Mike shook his head. "It's just a little package. You'd bring it to an apartment in Bangkok. There's nothing to it."

I thought about it for a moment. I'd almost given up ever learning more about their business. Now he was asking me to participate. "I don't know. I think I'd be too nervous," I told him.

"Not you. You'll be a pro."

"Well, what'll I be carrying?"

Mike looked off in the distance and took a deep breath. "Heroin."

I shook my head and laughed. "No way. I've seen *Midnight Express*."

Mike shrugged. "Why don't you think about it and see how you feel?"

Afterwards, I ducked into my room, but I was shaking. His offer meant they were starting to trust me. I thought that if I helped them out, I could make a place for myself in their weird family. There were risks, but I knew about them. I'd watched those men exist in that world they created, and I trusted that they knew what they were doing. In all the years they'd been working up there, they still hadn't been caught.

Yesterday, Jake took me up into a poppy field. Red and white flowers bobbed in a blanket of sunshine, their bright colors glistening from their round crêpe paper petals. The Thai farmer, who looked like a gangster in his sunglasses and jeans, stopped and knelt before one plant, proudly holding up the flower's head, its long piping neck, and thick pod above. He reached into his pocket and took out a sharp knife. I thought he was going to hurt us, but instead, he held the flower's stem between his index and middle finger and slit the pod; not cutting it off completely, just scoring it with a distinct mark. A milky white liquid emerged. Opium, Jake whispered as he quickly reached for a Marlboro and spread the ooze over the cigarette paper so that when he lit it up, dark smoke curled above the ashes. Then he handed it to me and I took a drag. The flowers seemed to tilt their heads nodding in the breeze.

It happened so quickly. I know that's no excuse. They gave me a map with directions to an apartment on Soi Cowboy. From there, someone else was supposed to take the stuff to another person who got it out of the country. The nationality of that second person depended on the economic climate. At the time, Nigeria was supplying most of the mules. Inside Bangkok's girlie bars, tall lean African men seemed to be enjoying the seediest of the city's pleasures, but what was really on their minds was the thousands of dollars they would make after completing one delivery of heroin. A fortune in their country.

I felt good. Before leaving Fang, Mrs. Chang read my tea leaves. I didn't tell her what I was doing, but she said it was safe to take a trip and predicted a big change was about to take place. I remember laughing, thinking, A big change? A big change had already occurred. In three months, I'd gone from being a college student to a drug courier living in the hills of Thailand.

The day before I left, I ran around trying to find something inconspicuous to wear. I forgot about my one good dress sitting creased at the bottom of my knapsack. It was too pretty to wear in dusty old Fang. The only problem was, when I put it on and glanced in the mirror, I looked like an animal out in the wild for too long. My skin was rough and dry, my lips cracked from the sun. The loose-fitting floral pattern didn't seem as if it belonged on someone as savage as me.

Mike nodded approvingly, but Jake wasn't happy to see me dressed that way at all. "Why don't you forget about this? You don't have to do it," he begged.

"What happens if I decide to leave Thailand? Without a visa, I'll never be able to get back in the country."

"Who's gonna check?"

"Leave her alone," Mike cut in. "Let her do what she wants. See how great she looks? Nothing's going to happen to her."

Minutes before the bus was due to leave, I hopped on Jake's bike and we drove down to the depot. An old man selling fresh fruit wheeled his cart over to us, as if just by seeing me he knew it was worth walking a few extra yards to make a sale. I bought a bunch of lichee, the stems crawling with tiny black ants, and peeled off the shell of each fruit, eating the white iridescent meat and letting the juice drip down between my fingers. Jake took my hand and started licking the sticky path while I slapped at the ants that had started following the sweet stream.

By then, I was familiar with the noises of the different forms of transportation and could practically predict what the conveyance would look like before I ever saw it. There were the *samlors*, the *songthaews*, the dirt bikes, and the mopeds, and I heard the bus sputtering down the road into town. For some reason, even though I'd arrived in Fang on a first-class air-conditioned bus, it was impossible to get out of town in such comfort. What came rumbling along was an old American export with rounded windows and a cracked windshield, and suddenly I felt frightened. Maybe it was the way Jake wouldn't say anything, or how I thought the other passengers were eyeing me as if they knew exactly what I was up to, but it was too late. I hoisted my bag over my shoulder and boarded the bus, maybe the most stupid, and yet bravest thing I've ever done.

The next morning I arrived in Bangkok before the sun had even risen. The air was smokey from the charcoal fires of the men and women who had set up stalls around the bus station, getting ready to serve steaming bowls of breakfast noodles, rice soup, and pork buns. I watched as shiny new "deluxe luxury" buses pulled into the station, opened their doors, and spewed out streams of conservatively dressed office workers who hurried into overcrowded city buses waiting at the curb.

Since I was back in the city, I tried to act like an American tourist again, clutching my bag, staring at a city map, then slowly heading out into the traffic. My whole system felt stunned, as if my body was getting a numbing jolt from the modern world: the cars, electricity, running water, and people dressed in Western clothing. I could have been some hill-tribe woman entering civilization for the first time.

I *tuk-tuked* over to Sukumvit, an area of fancy hotels and air-conditioned stores. Camouflaged between respectable businessmen, Japanese tourists, and Thai bureaucrats, I drank cappuccino at an expensive French café and thought of nothing but the tightly wrapped package inside a brown envelope deep at the bottom of my knapsack. I picked up the *Bangkok Post* lying on the next table and read the date. It was April 12th, exactly three months since I first arrived in Thailand.

When I finished my coffee, I caught another *tuk-tuk* over to Soi Cowboy. By then I'd been traveling nearly twenty-four hours and I guess I should have gotten a room, but I knew I couldn't relax until the delivery was complete and I was on my way to Malaysia. It was exciting. Thailand had become my home, and by visiting another country I was going to start my travels all over again.

Soi Cowboy was deserted. Because of the early hour, all the neon lights advertising nightclubs, dancing girls, and Karaoke bars were switched off. Trash and cigarette butts were the only evidence of the recently concluded night. I walked down the pavement hoping no one would notice me: a young American in a cotton sun dress, sandals, and knapsack—nothing unusual. The touts were all asleep, and the barkers had gone off to their day jobs. For all anyone knew, I was just another lamb who'd lost her way.

The address was easy to find, and I climbed up a flight of wooden stairs, smelling the stale smoke and spilt beer from the nightclub below. It was easy to sense that anyone living in that building had to be involved in drugs or prostitution, but after I knocked and a young man opened the door, I saw that families lived there too. Behind the man stood a Thai woman, dressed in traditional sarong and blouse, cradling an infant wrapped to her chest, with a toddler holding onto her leg. Seeing me, she quickly gathered up her children and herded them into a back room.

"Enter, enter," the guy named Lek urged. He was slim and attractive and spoke English well. "Do not worry. They told me you were coming, so there is no need to be frightened."

"I guess I'm just not used to doing this kind of thing," I mumbled, slipping off my shoes and stepping into the empty room. The plan had been so simple when I first went over it in Fang, but once he started examining me closer, I began to tremble.

He closed the door and bent down to open the knapsack. When he took out the package, I thought our deal was complete and began to gather my things, but he put out his hand to stop me. "It's always good to know what you're carrying."

I wanted to get as far away from that stuff as possible, but he was grinning, waiting for me to respond.

"Is she your wife?" I asked, nodding towards the other room where the woman and children had disappeared.

He shrugged, as if to say the girl was his wife, but he had no idea how it had happened. "You are enjoying all of Thailand's pleasures?" He looked at me intently. I'd begun to notice many Thais had this way about them, as if they were omniscient and knew exactly what I was thinking.

Then there was a knock on the door, and we glanced at each other. For a moment, I thought I saw a cloud of worry cross his face as he motioned for me to get into the back room with the rest of his family. I grabbed my bag and slipped into the corner where the Thai woman was already crouched with her infant and the other one huddled between her knees. Squeezing my eyes shut, I tried to imagine myself one of her children protected just by being near her.

The hall door creaked as Lek opened up and my stomach turned. I expected to hear Interpol agents come storming through the doorway with their handcuffs and loud voices, but he started whispering to someone in English instead. Behind me, his wife began making disapproving clucking sounds with her tongue as she pushed me out in front of her and we all emerged from the little room. Lek glanced in our direction and looked embarrassed, then turned back to the girl standing in front of him. It was Cara Duryeye. I recognized her right away. With her cropped hair and earrings running up the side of her ear, she was hard to mistake.

Lek gestured to his wife to get back into the room and spoke angrily to her in Thai. She answered with sweeping motions that included me as well as Cara. I pushed between the two of them wanting to catch up with Cara, who had turned and dashed down the stairs. "Maddy. Cara," Lek called from the top of the landing.

By the time I reached the street, Cara had disappeared.

When I told Jake I was only going to be away for a couple of days, I hadn't meant to lie. My plan was to cross the border at Hat Yai, get my passport stamped, and catch the next train back in the other direction, but once I left Bangkok I found I enjoyed being on my own with no one critiquing the way I was acting or telling me how I should behave. After all those weeks of being away from home, I no longer felt self-conscious or worried that something terrible was going to happen. I was on my way to Malaysia, a completely different country, and if I just relaxed I knew I'd enjoy the trip. I rationalized it this way: leaving Jake alone for a while would give him a chance to see what it was like without me. He wasn't going anywhere, and I would be back with him soon enough. So once on board the train to Malaysia, I let a group of British and Australian travelers convince me to go along with them to Penang.

They were a happy bunch. They'd been staying on Ko Samui, an island off southern Thailand, and were still dressed as if they were about to spend another day on the beach. The women wore bikini tops, sarong skirts, and flip-flops. The guys were unshaven and had on cut-off jeans and worn T-shirts. One was only wearing a bathrobe, as if he'd been heading for the shower when someone suggested he come along for the ride.

Before we crossed the border, they lit up the remainder of their weed and blew the smoke out the open window, just as we passed Malaysia's welcoming signs at the frontier. Signs that read DADA = DEATH; the punishment for smuggling drugs into the country. I remember giggling as the border patrol looked for our luggage and gazed into our glazed eyes, fully aware that we were another group of stoned *farangs*. Of course, the officers didn't find anything on us and had to let us pass. Then for the next hour or so, we traded stories about the places we'd been. They told me about the islands, the beach huts, the drugs, and the all-night parties. I described northern Thailand, and its jungle remoteness. I never mentioned Jake or Fang or heroin.

Once in Penang, we all checked into the New World Hostel, a great white colonial mansion with large windows, wooden verandas, and a musty odor. It seemed as if all the upholstery and bed coverings hadn't been changed since the nineteen-fifties, when the British gave the country back to the Malays. Many other travelers were staying there too. Most came to renew their visas and remained a few days. They did a bit of shopping, drank beer, then returned to Thailand where some were living on beaches, working at language schools, or raising families up in the mountains. We all looked the same: wild-eyed, emaciated, and tanned to the color of braised beef. If it wasn't for the busloads of tourists from Europe, Japan, and the States, the Malaysians would have had every reason to believe that all Westerners were a bunch of drug-addicted hippies in need of a bath. But throughout the city there were also groups of well-fed tourists spending a few nights at a five star hotel, exploring the botanic gardens and other remnants of the colonial era; getting their pictures taken holding pythons or baby monitor lizards; then traveling on to the next destination like Kuala Lumpur or Singapore.

Since Malaysia was a former British colony, most Malaysians spoke English and there were many people to talk to. The young students—especially the males—liked to practice their English with me, and the travelers who hadn't been to Thailand yet had many questions to ask. Suddenly, I became the expert. I'd sit at tea stalls near the hotel chatting for hours to whomever came by. Everyone wanted to know about Bangkok, Chiang Mai, Ko Sumet, and other popular backpacker destinations. I never mentioned Fang, the drugs, or the Western prisoners. They could find out about that for themselves. And although Mrs. Chang might have paid me a good commission for bringing more guests to her motel, I knew the guys would be annoyed to see an increase in the number of travelers wandering through the gates.

I kept meaning to go down to the railroad station to reserve a ticket back to Bangkok, but I never seemed to end up there. I was down to my last few hundred dollars. In Fang, Mike had promised me several thousand baht for the delivery. Without that, I wouldn't be able to keep the room at Mrs. Chang's, and I didn't know what I'd do if I didn't have money. I considered moving in with Jake. After all, we spent so much time together, it was a waste not to share a room, but I had the feeling he wasn't going to be too eager to do something like that. Right from the start, the age difference meant a lot to him. He used to joke about it, reminding me that by the time I turned thirty, he'd be an old man, and I think that sort of flipped him out. I kept telling him that I wasn't looking to get married, but I don't think he believed me.

Yesterday was an auspicious day. I read about it in the newspaper. On the front page of the New Straits Times there was a photograph of a happy Chinese couple: the girl wore a traditional Western bridal gown; the man was in a tuxedo. They both stood proudly in front of a white, four door Mercedes sedan that had been wrapped in a large red bow. N-E-1-4 MARRIAGE, the caption read. The article said that everyone who's Chinese and wants to get married must book appointments for auspicious days. For the next three weeks, only inauspicious days are left for unlucky brides and grooms. The Chinese would rather wait another year than get married on one of these bad luck days. I don't blame them. Whoever gets married needs all the luck in the world.

A few months ago, I might have hoped that Ben and I would get married. I know that sounds weird, but who doesn't wonder if her boyfriend will be the one she might be spending the rest of her life with? I think if everyone who wanted to get married was forced to take a trip around the world with her prospective partner, there'd be fewer wrecked marriages right from the start. Did Ben and I have to come thousands of miles just to split up? I guess so, but I'm grateful to him for going on this trip with me.

*C*ongratulations, Maddy! You finally got off your ass and bought a ticket back to Bangkok. Yeah! If everything goes well, I'll be in Fang in less than three days. I miss Jake. I'm here alone, but it's nice knowing there's someone who cares about me who's not too far away.

A Muslim woman was sitting behind the ticket counter at the train station. She smiled from beneath her veil, as if with every long-distance ticket she sold, she was taking that journey herself. The way she was dressed, covered from head to toe, made me feel lucky to be from the West. How much of our life happens by chance? Why wasn't I born into a culture where I had to hide myself like a dirty secret, marry the man my family picked out for me, and work like a slave to keep him happy? Here I am, free to travel indefinitely, while other women around the world are hauling bricks on their heads or being set on fire because their families can't provide enough dowry.

No one seemed sad about my departure. The beautiful Chinese desk clerk pulled my bill from her files, added up the charges, and presented it to me. The total was three times as much as any guesthouse in Thailand, even though the Thai guesthouses were much cleaner and more comfortable. My train didn't leave until late that night, so I stashed my bag beneath the counter and went down to the tea stall to see who I'd find there.

The only empty seat was at a table occupied by a single woman. She looked familiar, and when she turned around, I recognized Annemarie.

"We thought you'd gone home, but you are here," Annemarie cried, jumping up from her chair.

I searched the steam-filled room for Brigid, but Annemarie shook her head. "We split up. Don't you know?"

"What are you doing here?"

"Same as you, I suppose."

"I'm going back tonight."

Annemarie shrugged. "I just arrived."

"How's Chiang Mai?"

"No different. People come and people go."

"What about Bernd?"

Her mouth turned down. "I have stopped visiting him and that is what bothered Brigid. I told her that I could no longer be married to this person behind bars. He is what you call a hopeless case. All he cares about is junk and more junk. It got to be he was living a better life inside than we were out. We were always so worried about him and how he was doing."

"What about Brigid?"

"She cannot do much. She brings him what he needs, but he doesn't care anymore. I feel for him, but he also disgusts me."

"And Eric?"

"He is no better, but I think your government has arranged for him to go home. And do you remember Jake? He is gone too. We haven't seen him for weeks."

I took a sip of sweet tea, wanting to take some time to think how much to tell her, but she continued. "He was a big drug smuggler, you know? He even asked maybe we take some heroin back to Frankfurt for him, but we told him 'no.' I haven't seen him since. It's so obvious now that he's gone. We could have gotten into a lot of trouble. He treated us like we were two stupid little girls."

As she talked, I remembered picking up the *International Herald Tribune* and seeing a grainy photograph of two British teenagers who'd just been busted at Don Muang with a couple of kilos of dope in their luggage. The article explained how they had used their small savings to come to Thailand because they heard the country was "a real laugh." Sometime during their holiday, they met a man who asked them to do him a favor, and they could make a few quid. Until that moment, I imagined the man to be some unsavory character from the Thai mafia or an international drug cartel. I never thought he could be Mike, or Pete, or even Jake.

Neither of us wanted to spend the rest of the day sitting around the tea stall. Besides, it was going to be my last chance to see the city, so we decided to visit Penang Hill, a place I'd read about in a glossy travel brochure.

The city heat wasn't as oppressive as it was in Bangkok, and the streets were a lot less crowded, so we moved quickly between food vendors and clothing stalls to a downtown shopping center where large movie posters had been slapped against concrete walls, advertising upcoming films like *Alien II, Robocop*, and other gruesome Hollywood movies that were so bad they'd never come out in the States.

Inside the air-conditioned mall, Malay women window

shopped. They were dressed in shimmering satin slacks with matching tunics of rich scarlet, emerald, amber, and black. The women's eyes twinkled playfully from behind their head scarves, and I started to understand how much they could enjoy themselves. They didn't need Levis or tight tank tops to make them feel sexy. Their dress was respected by the men, who didn't dare call out or proposition them, as they seemed able to do to us.

I tried to understand the different cultural attitudes toward sex. In Thailand, where sex was a booming business, I was able to wear anything I liked and walked around freely without being accosted by rude remarks or comments. In Penang, that changed. A woman was a whore if the tip of her elbow poked out from beneath her blouse, or her veil didn't cover her entire head. But I was a Westerner; my skin was white. Even if I presented myself in purdah, people would have stared at me anyway.

We found the bus that took us to the foot of the mountain where a funicular would transport us farther up to the gardens above the city. School was just letting out and little boys and girls swarmed onto the bus, staring and giggling as they pushed past us down the aisle. The bus slowly emptied as it lurched up the winding streets, until there were only a few children on board. Every now and then, I caught the driver's bloodshot eyes in his rearview mirror. He quickly glanced back to the road with an expression that made my skin crawl. It was not curious or innocent like the way the children examined us. He seemed to think we owed him something more than the fare we paid for the ride.

At the top of the hill, the bus came to a halt and the remaining passengers piled off. We glanced outside our window to where there was a line of identical green-and-white city buses parked at a turn-around. Our driver cut the engine, got up, and motioned to a booth selling tickets for the train just a few blocks ahead. Annemarie rose first and started toward the back, but the driver didn't open the door. "Last stop," he called out.

Neither of us knew what he meant. Since we were the only passengers left, he could do whatever he liked and no one would ever know. When we turned around to the front door, he stood in the aisle blocking our way. "You must have guide to show you hill," he sneered, popping a wad of betel nut into his mouth.

He reminded me of a giant hawk who, at any moment, could swoop down and capture us in his sharp talons, and carry us away. I shook my head and tried to edge by him.

"Penang Hill is very dangerous without guide," he warned again.

"We'll decide later," Annemarie stammered. "Now, if you please, we want to get off."

He looked offended, but didn't remove himself from the aisle. "There are many bad men around."

"If you care so much, you should let us pass," I told him, looking out the windshield to see if there was anyone who could come to our aid. There were only the other drivers drinking glasses of tea at a nearby stall.

Our driver smiled again, nodded his head a few times, and motioned with his arm. "Of course, you may pass. Would I not allow you to pass?"

Once he moved aside, Annemarie took her first steps down the stairs onto the sidewalk. She was safe there, but I was still looking into the driver's demonic eyes. He wasn't a big man, but I could tell he was after me. I didn't have much choice, so I stretched out my arms in front of my chest like a battering ram. Just as he lunged, I blocked his way and shoved him back into his seat.

"Run," Annemarie shouted, and we dashed down the curving lanes that spread out from the top of the ridge. My heart was pounding, but the momentum of running downhill kept my legs moving. I wasn't going to stop until I reached safety.

At the bottom, we came to a market where the streets were lined with vendors selling cuts of meat, eggs, and live chickens. "What did he want?" Annemarie gasped.

"How should I know? People must go up to that hill everyday."

"It's like we're food for them when there's no other man accompanying us. What if he caught us? What would he have done?"

"Probably nothing. Maybe he just wanted to touch our skin."

Annemarie sighed. "I know it sounds horrid, but I feel so much better when there are other tourists around. When there are no tourists, *you* become the sight."

We started toward the esplanade along the bay, somewhere safe and familiar. All along the pathways, women had set up charcoal pits and were selling skewers of chicken, beef, and fish. The air was smoky and warm. In the distance, the water from the bay sparkled and lapped against the stone wall.

"How long are you planning to stay?" I asked as we sat on the seawall and watched the muddy tide drift in.

"In Penang?"

"No. In Thailand. Don't you ever want to go home?"

Annemarie considered this as if she were having trouble even remembering where home was. Finally she said, "I think people leave their homes because they're tired of the way things are, and if they go back, they don't want it all to be the same again."

"When I left the States, I didn't think about it. I was with my boyfriend, and we were just going to travel. I didn't have any idea what that really meant. Now everything's changed. I'm doing shit I never would have imagined."

Annemarie nodded. "It's not the same here. You're forced to change."

"I can't decide if that's good or bad. I mean, I know it's good, but don't you ever feel scared? Everything from before means so little to me now."

"Is that bad?"

"Do you ever wonder what'll happen when you go home?"

"Germany will always be there. I don't have to worry about that. The saddest part is that *you* may change, but everything at home stays the same: your friends, your family. You'll see. Every summer, when I was a teenager, I got together with some friends and went all over Europe by rail. It was kind of crazy, but we loved it. We slept in the trains and on the floors of the stations. We ate whatever food we could find. It was as if we were suddenly poor, you know, without a home. Then, when our train passes ran out, we'd go back to being regular kids again. Since then, I've always felt grateful I had such an experience. It's become easier to make any place home, even if it's the floor of a railway station."

"Didn't your parents care how you were living?"

"They couldn't imagine. They thought we were staying

in hostels and such, but we didn't want to waste our money. I am one of five children. They were just happy to see I was surviving and they could give their attention to the next in line."

"My mom has always let me do almost anything I wanted, but she'd be here tomorrow if she knew."

"Americans are different. In Europe, not everyone wants so much for their children."

"What do you think happened to Jake?"

She looked at me strangely. "How would I know about him?"

"You said he's a big drug dealer."

"'Smuggler' is what I said. He pays people to carry the heroin back to their countries. He offered us ten thousand marks. That isn't a lot you know, not for risking your life."

"I thought he was your friend."

"Don't worry. We can't get in trouble for hanging around him. Anyway, he's gone now."

"Yeah," I said weakly, thinking about our rooms up in Fang.

That night, before my train left, I slipped into a phone stall to call my mother. When I first told her I was going to Thailand, she told me that I'd enjoy the trip better if I knew what I was doing. I told her *traveling* was what I was doing. Now I needed to talk to someone who knew me before I took the trip. I bought five minutes on a phone card. Five minutes seemed right because it wouldn't give us enough time to say much of anything. When the phone started ringing, I suddenly felt nauseous. I remembered how her voice always quivered with concern, as if she were silently listening on the other end to hear explanations for questions she was afraid to ask. By the fourth ring, I hung up. As usual, there was too much to explain.

It's funny how with memory, episodes in your life speed up like cuts in a movie. There is always action where you are *doing* something, but what happens to all those other moments in between: the hours spent staring into space, wondering about your future, regretting bad decisions, or eavesdropping on other people's conversations? All that has not been adequately captured here. Don't be mistaken. Traveling is not like a continuous drama. There are hours of unencumbered time: the long bus journeys, the vacant moments sitting around the guesthouses, the endless gassy beers at traveler bars, or lying in bed in a hot, stuffy room because you have nothing better to do.

I returned to Chiang Mai too exhausted to get on another bus and head farther north. By then, I felt as if I drove over another bump, my head would explode. I needed to find a place to rest, somewhere to set my bags and lie horizontal. But everything in the city seemed so strange. I'd only been away for a month, but in that short time it was as if the whole place had changed. Even Lilly's Guesthouse, where Ben and I first stayed, seemed different. The garden, which had once been filled with travelers, was deserted; the waiter was new. The bulletin board still held notices and postcards sent to long-departed guests, and newer signs posting the rates for each room, along with check-in and check-out times. At the front desk, I asked about

Brigid, but the desk clerk didn't understand. "Monsoon no good. Many tourists go."

I looked up at the bright blue sky. It'd been hot as hell most of the day.

"You see," he told me, "you be swimming in streets this afternoon."

My head was buzzing with thoughts of Jake and what I was going to do when I got back to Fang. I no longer trusted my instincts or judgment and hoped I could find someone who knew me before I met him. Sometimes, those kind of people can provide an accurate reflection of the way you're behaving and give perspective to how you see things. If I didn't find someone like that soon, I thought I would lose my mind.

I made my way along the river to Lucky Lady, hoping to catch Juliette, but the bar was dark and deserted. The silver poles stretched straight up to the ceiling; the cool chrome smudged by the palms of the girls who slithered up and down on them the night before. It didn't seem like anyone was there, but I tried calling out. At last the patter of footsteps came down the hall and the same old woman appeared, wearing a halter top and tight black slacks. Wrinkles of fat fell in layers over her cinched waistband. "We close now. You come back another time," she told me.

"But I'm looking for Juliette, one of the dancers."

The woman shook her head. "We no have dancers here."

"I'm looking for a French girl. Her name is Juliette."

The woman shook her head again. "French girl? No have."

This was a typical Thai remark. Even though all the evidence was to the contrary, she thought that if she said it again, I would believe it.

"She works for Mr. Tam."

The woman puckered up her lips. "Mr. Tam? Mr. Tam, who?"

Okay. She won. "Well, if you meet someone named Juliette, tell her Maddy came to see her."

The woman shrugged. "Sorry, no Juliette here."

I passed through the heavy drapes and into the bright sunlight. I was going to have to keep looking for Juliette myself.

I ended up walking by the prison and thought of the men inside who'd once been ordinary travelers, like I was. Maybe they'd just finished college, or were on breaks between jobs, drifting in some harmless way. Now I was beginning to understand how an innocent trip could turn out so wrong.

The reception area at Shangri-La was empty, and no one questioned me as I walked through the garden and upstairs to the second floor, where a line of washing hung out to dry: a string of panties, a bra, and some colorful blouses. The door to Juliette's room was shut and the window slats closed, but I knocked anyway, listening to my tapping echo through the courtyard. At last there was some movement and the door opened slowly. Juliette appeared wrapped in a purple-and-green sarong, her hand shielding her eyes from the sun. "Who is there?"

"It's me. Maddy."

"*Qui?*"

"I used to live next door."

She shifted around so the sun's glare wasn't directly in her eyes. "You," she exclaimed. "So you have come back?"

I edged toward her room, not wanting to talk on the terrace, but she put herself in my way.

"Did I wake you?"

She smiled and rubbed her eyes. "Yes. Is it late?"

"Only about three in the afternoon."

She pushed her hair back and stretched. "That's good. I needed to sleep. Work has been insane, you know. So many businessmen."

"You must be making a lot of money."

She sighed. "Money comes and money goes. My life isn't cheap. But why have you returned?"

"Have you seen Brigid?"

She shook her head. "I do not see many Westerners now. Only the ones who come to the club. Then, they don't want to see me. They're more interested in the Asian girls. Girls like me, they can have for free."

"I thought you were going to quit."

She shrugged. "Oh no. We have many Japanese coming in. I can't be with each one of them."

Noises came from behind the door. Someone else was in the room, but obviously she wanted to keep whoever it was hidden. "Can we meet downstairs?" she whispered.

At the front desk, I ordered an orange juice and pancakes and watched two Australian women waiting to rent mopeds. They looked gorgeous and full of good health. The sun had given them orange freckles that spread across their faces and ran into their streaked blond hair. They talked loudly about how drunk they'd gotten the night before. "Barbara must have had her head up her arse. Did you see the way she was coming on to that bloke?"

"He was Italian, right?"

"Italian my arse. He was bloody American."

"She's desperate to win Fuck-Me Bingo. She only needs to bonk an Italian and she'll fill her card."

They giggled loudly, and I let their conversation drift over me. Before I heard much more, their mopeds were brought around and they hoisted their long legs over the saddles, revved the engines, and sped off. Their vacation was progressing a lot better than mine. How was it that *I* was the one who'd gotten caught up in something completely dangerous and illegal?

Juliette arrived and ordered a Nescafé. Without her makeup and exotic clothing, she looked tired and plain.

"The last time I saw you, you were on your way to Fang," she remembered. "I should go there sometime, *non?*"

"It's just another town."

"But you like it there?"

I nodded and asked about the prison.

"*Merci a dieu* I don't have to think about that anymore. How terrible it was. I am happy not to have to worry about what day it is, or if I will get there on time. It was always so difficult for me to wake up."

Juliette seemed different, too. If she hadn't been describing her life of topless dancing and prostitution, she could have been telling me about her week at the *bourse* in Paris or the rigors of classes at the Sorbonne. When I first met her, I thought she was so independent. Now I saw she was like any other working woman. Fucking men for money was just another job.

"Do you ever think about going home?" I asked.

She puffed out her cheeks in that quintessential French way, as if only the French could ever feel so bored or despondent. "What do I have to go home to? I am twenty-eight years old. It's too late to return to school. I'm not going to be a sales girl or work in an office building. I can get a job dancing in Amsterdam, but the weather is much better here."

"Doesn't anyone miss you?"

"Does anyone miss *you*?"

"I tried calling my mother, but she wasn't home."

"*Á bien.*"

"It's strange, but I don't really miss anyone either. I guess maybe I should."

"You've only been here a few months or so. The longer you're gone, the further away that other life seems, and I am happy for that."

I kept quiet and wished I could feel as content as she was. When I looked up, she was staring at me. "You do not look well. You are not sick again?"

"I just feel so messed up," I told her. I was hungry, sunstroked, and exhausted from too much travel, but I also felt as if I had this intense sorrow crowding out my insides.

"Maybe you'd like something to make you feel better," she offered, gently touching my hand. "I think I know what you need."

I wasn't sure what she meant. Noodles? Rice? Alcohol? Drugs? Whatever it was, I was ready to take it, and the fact that someone was willing to provide it for me made it all the more appealing. I'd already seen how quickly pain could be erased. Sometimes, before I went to sleep, I wished I could return to that moment when Ben and I first touched down at Don Muang and I was sitting next to him, gripping his wrist as the plane skidded to a halt on the tarmac, and I imagined the surge of adrenaline rippling through his body into mine. At that time, we were so connected. I never wondered how he was feeling. And that first evening, as we walked wide-eyed through Khao San Road, we thought we'd arrived in some kind of magical Never Never Land.

Whoever had been in Juliette's room was gone by the time we got back there. She began searching for something in her drawer. When I saw her take out a small plastic bag and pour yellowish powder out onto a book cover on the table, I shook my head. I'd never tried heroin, and I didn't want to start. There was something so final about addiction, like the poison never left you, and I was scared of that.

"But you must try," she laughed. "It is nothing to worry about. No one gets hurt by sniffing a little. The real danger comes if you use a needle. You must promise never to do that."

I remembered Lek telling me that I needed to know what I was carrying. Then there was Juliette looking at me with her beautiful hazel eyes, and I felt like a virgin, both eager and afraid. If I did it with her, I knew I'd be safe.

"Relax," she insisted as she cut up the lines and bent over the table. I shut my eyes and followed her example, snorting up the powder and feeling the tiny granules hit the back of my nose. Then I waited for something to happen.

Soon, I became a tree rooted to the ground. Above me was my trunk thick with branches reaching out in all directions. The wind whistled through my leaves. Below, the roots grabbed harder at the gritty earth; rutted fists clutching the certainty of the ground. I watched as my leaves dropped, circling in the wind, then swirling up into the air and gently drifting down again, their golden undersides shimmering with each gust. I giggled with them, but then they got caught up with another burst and scattered again.

I have no idea what really happened. After a while, I think I was in some kind of dream state, my mind slowly coming down like the leaves I saw inside my head. Whenever I felt the high leaving me, I squeezed my eyelids shut and tried to recapture the buoyancy, but that sensation slowly ebbed away. I was still waiting for my imagination to whisk me off again, when I looked out the window and realized that the sky had turned dark. I was in Juliette's room with no idea where she went, or if I was ever going to get back to Fang.

At this point, my world was becoming as interconnected as routes on a road map. I was no longer so surprised at coincidences. I caught a bus up north and arrived in Fang late at night. The houses in town were dark; the inhabitants asleep. As I walked in the low moonlight, a slight breeze blew, sending dry leaves tumbling down the dirt road ahead of me. I watched as their shadows seemed to reach out toward one another and then spin away. I felt as though those leaves were like me, reaching out trying to catch hold of something just out of grasp.

I was returning more than a week late. What did they think happened to me? Maybe they suspected I ripped them off, sold their dope, and made off with the money. Why not? I guess I could have telephoned, but using modern technology to call someone in a developing country never crossed my mind.

The iron gate squeaked as I pushed it open. Across the courtyard, the soda machine, with its glowing red Coca-Cola sign, sat sentry along side Mrs. Chang's door. From the skeletal shadows of the dirt bikes glistening in the moonlight, I knew the guys were home, but I wanted to wait until I calmed down before seeing them.

Inside, my room smelled of lime or pine spray; some artificial air freshener meant to give the impression that the place had been cleaned. A pile of clothes Mrs. Chang had just washed lay neatly on my bed. The towels had been replaced, and it even looked as though the rug had been swept. I took my time. I needed to think. Despite the cleanliness and order, I felt something else had changed up there too.

From the other side of the wall, I could hear the men's voices, low and husky. Of course, they were still awake. They rarely slept. It was as if the war was still raging close to home. They needed to continue plotting, strategizing, planning their next action.

"They're searching every bag at Don Muang," I heard Mike grumble.

"It's because of those British cunts. Now they're gonna think every chick with a passport is smuggling," Pete added. "And we got this other one working for us. We should have found a guy. Didn't you say she has a boyfriend?"

"He's not in the picture," Jake answered.

"Well, Cara should lay low. She's been at it for too long."

"Fuck you," a woman's voice cut in. "I'm good at what I do."

"We're gonna send Maddy again, if she ever gets back," Mike said. "Your job is to make sure she doesn't fuck up like she's doing now."

"Maddy will come back," Jake insisted. "And when she does, Cara's gonna make friends."

"I don't give a fuck," Cara replied. "You can make me babysit whoever the hell you want and I'll still move more shit than any of you. I'm goddamn invisible."

The others laughed. When I was ready, I walked straight into that room, wanting to get the worst over, and there they were, staring at me like I'd dropped down from outer space. The only person I remember seeing clearly was Cara, sitting on the floor, her legs folded alongside her, a cigarette dangling between her fingers.

"Well, would you look who's back," Jake called out.

I tried to smile, but I couldn't even look at him.

"How'd things go?" Mike asked.

Jake pulled me down to sit with him on the bed and squeezed my hand. "You've been away awhile."

"I went to Penang."

He grinned, as if he liked the fact that I'd done something on my own, but the whole while he was sitting next to me, I was watching Cara smoke. Maybe she was weaned too early or just needed something to stick in her mouth, but she inhaled the way kids sucked on pacifiers, where their cheeks pinched in and their eyes closed tight, as if she was in some sort of ecstatic trance. Then, when she exhaled, her body relaxed and she looked beatific and calm.

"I saw your picture on Khao San Road," I told her.

She coughed and opened her eyes wide, blowing smoke directly into my face. "Fucking parents. If they think I'm gonna be hauled back to California, they're out of their minds."

"Those posters kind of scared me."

"Well, they shouldn't have. My mom is nuts. She's probably driving up and down the coast right now giving lectures about what a fuck up I am. I used to run away a lot. Coming after me is her career. It's what she *does.*"

"I never had the nerve to run away."

"Yeah. Well, I was desperate. I might as well have been born an orphan. The whole time I lived with my mom, I felt like a wolf being raised by fucking rabbits. Their idea of living wasn't mine."

Then Cara stopped talking and sighed, as if she didn't want to go on, but that was how she began most of her stories. Her life consisted of a succession of slights and disappointments handed to her by people she once loved. "I was thirteen," she continued, leaning back against the bed and staring into the smoke-filled room, as if she were narrating some imaginary movie. "Mom and my stepfather, Don, took the car down to Santa Barbara and didn't even bother asking me if I wanted to go along. They always did stuff like that. I didn't exist until I pissed them off. Anyway, when I woke up, the house was empty, but the smells from their stinking life were still all around: coffee grounds, Don's aftershave, the lemon body wash my mom wore. The two of them made me sick. Don supported us, so Mom had this idea that she had to do all the housework. Whenever Don was home, she was always hurrying around with the vacuum cleaner trailing at her heels. But she was a chameleon. Once, she showed me a photograph of herself back in the sixties. She was at a party where everyone had long hair and these wasted smiles. She was sitting across the laps of three men. One of them was my father.

"After the sixties, she had me and must've decided that marriage to some rich idiot was what she needed to survive. It took her five years to find Don. She probably had to tell him some wild story to make up for her hippie days because he's one big square. You should see him. He always wears the same clothes. On weekdays, it's a dark blue suit and tie, like some hot-shit businessman. On weekends, it's his one pair of discount jeans and a polo shirt. Don't men look stupid in discount jeans?"

I stared at her. She took some time to raise a bottle of beer to her lips, but then, when she did, she chugged it down. I wanted her to finish her story so I could be alone with Jake, but she had this unwieldy narrative running through her head.

"The day I first left home, I watched TV until the afternoon when only golf and cooking shows were on. After a while, I got hungry and looked into the refrigerator where there were all these neatly wrapped packages: carrot sticks, American cheese, and cucumber slices. My mom loved her food processor. After shopping, she took the fruits and vegetables—everything that could be sliced, diced, and julienned—and put them in the Cuisinart. Once they were chopped, she stuffed them into Ziploc bags. She was crazy about Ziplocs. She even put cartons of milk in them.

"In school, we were reading these books about running away, people who just picked up and left: *Grapes of Wrath*, *Of Mice and Men*. I don't know why they give books like that to ninth graders. They make you feel if things get bad, you can always hit the road. On the afternoon that I'm talking about, I was sick of it all and went into my room to pack some clothes in a knapsack. I wanted them to come home and find their goddamn house empty. Then they'd see how much they missed me.

"So I took BART into the city. When I got off downtown, I was afraid that if I stood still, people would think I had no place to go. Outside the station, there was this wet fog that was so thick, I could barely see the buildings in front of me, and I followed a bunch of tourists who got onto a cable car. We ended up down by Fisherman's Wharf. The place was charged. There were all kinds of people pushing in and out of restaurants and clothing stores. Everyone seemed so fucking happy. I couldn't believe that while I'd been sitting around at home with nothing to do, all this other shit was going on."

"I always hated going down there," I told her.

"Well, I was hyped. I could hardly breathe. I must have walked up and down the wharf four or five times before I found a place to sit and just watch everyone go by. The people seemed to be from all over the world and were speaking different languages. I felt like this weirdo. What the hell was wrong with me? Why wasn't I happy like they were? But then I saw this other group. They weren't with their families or dressed in fancy clothing. They stood in the shadows like me.

"A few minutes later, one of them came over. He was just a kid, and he asked if I had a cigarette. At first I was frightened. My parents were always warning me about how dangerous the city was, like it was hell and they knew I'd end up there. It was no wonder I thought the guy was going to rob me—just grab my knapsack and run off like some thief on TV—but that wasn't what happened. He was nice and even introduced himself. I gave him some fake name like Stacy or Tracy. He called himself Sunset because that was the neighborhood he came from, but he said the place was more like Foghell.

"To those other tourists on the wharf, we could have been a brother and sister having a nice conversation while our parents finished dinner at one of the restaurants nearby. But they probably never saw the bottle of Jack Daniels sitting between us. The Jack tasted great. By then, I'd stolen so many shots from Don's liquor cabinet, I hardly noticed the alcohol going down. The mist had moved off the coast and the air turned cold. Across the water in Sausalito, tiny lights flickered far away in the darkness."

"You make it sound so exciting."

She smirked, as if there was something she was keeping secret. "It *was* fucking exciting. That was when I first found out how great it was to be free. No parents, no teachers, no one telling me what to do."

"Did you stay out all night?"

She shook her head. "Sunset asked if I liked calamari and took me around to some  stalls that sold shit like crab legs, steamers, and corn on the cob. I prayed he wasn't going to make me go into any of the restaurants because I didn't have that kind of money, but we ended up near a vendor who sold fried squid, and we watched as people bought their food, then sat down to eat at counters nearby. Nobody ate everything. When they were finished, they just dumped their containers into the garbage cans, and Sunset ran to scoop them out before other junk was tossed on top. So there we were, eating those expensive meals for free.

"By then the temperature had turned cold. The fog began rolling in again, and my clothes were getting damp. I was tired too. You know how you feel when you just run out of energy and all you want to do is sleep in your own bed? I knew the trains shut down late, and I kept thinking, if I hurried, I'd be able to catch the last one. I asked Sunset if he was going back to his house, but he shook his head. He said he was home already.

"The train was filled with people who'd been out

partying all night. They were laughing and fooling around, but I ignored them, and got off at the end of the line. The neighborhood was quiet, like a set for some scary movie where the ax murderer is hiding behind the next tree. There wasn't a clue that anything else was going on in the world, and I wondered what Sunset was doing.

"When I stepped into my house, I felt safe, but I also had this feeling that I never should have come back. I was just putting something off that I'd have to do all over again."

Cara stopped talking for a moment, and I examined her closely. Maybe it was the drugs, or the effects of the life she was describing, but she seemed like a shell of a building: hard and empty. Whatever had once been inside her, had all been bombed out, and I was relieved when Jake came over and put his arm around me. "You girls have a lot to talk about?"

"Just stories," Cara told him.

He glanced at Cara and cocked his head. "She likes telling stories," he said, winking at me. "Sometimes she won't shut up. I'm going to bed. You coming?" He reached out and pulled me up. I nodded and followed him out the door.

The rains started the next day. There was so much mud no one could get up or down the mountains, so we all stayed in our rooms drinking whiskey, smoking opium, and playing Scrabble. I always beat them at Scrabble. Everyone had been together for so long, their vocabulary was very limited. Sometimes I refused to play because it only got them mad. When I'd win, I'd lose my friends for the rest of the day, and they were the only friends I had.

Mrs. Chang proved she truly was not a native of the countryside who was used to braving the monsoons. As soon as the rains began, she vacated the compound to visit relatives in the city of Sukhothai, leaving us in charge, claiming that there was little chance any other travelers would arrive. Of course, she was right.

One night, we had nothing to do. Pete was outside in his rain gear patching a flat on his motorbike. Mike was lying on his bed reading a *People* magazine that he must have read twenty times before. Cara was listening to a tape on her Walkman. The rain had come down so hard all day, no one had even gone into town to buy food and we were all feeling hungry. It was no secret where Mrs. Chang kept her rice and eggs; all we had to do was break into her apartment to use her stove. I was against it. She trusted us. But the guys became determined. Soon it was a game. They pushed at the windows and doors to her rooms, looking for a place to get in.

"She's got this place closed up tighter than a nun's twat," Mike yelled, shoving his full weight against the door frame. "What's she got in there anyway?"

"You know how Chinks are," Pete answered. "We're going to have to break something."

I backed away, thinking that Mrs. Chang might have had her own agenda with us, but that didn't mean we could bust into her property. I looked to Jake for help, hoping he'd side with me. Just as Mike was about to pry the wooden window slats apart with his long hunting knife, Jake knocked the blade out of his hand.

"What the fuck?" Mike spit.

"You're going to break into an old lady's house because you're too much of a pussy to go into town in the rain?"

"Cool it," Pete warned them both.

I didn't like where the argument was going. I could tell that they'd soon be fighting about bad judgment and then something uglier would come up.

"You always get everything your way," Mike accused.

"Suck my cock," Jake shot back.

"Why don't you let your girlfriend do that."

I turned around and ran back to my room, the screen door slamming behind me. The rain had soaked through my clothes and hair. Soon, Jake was standing in the doorway, a lit cigarette between his lips. "Fucking rain," he muttered. "Last year we practically killed each other. They can all go to hell."

"Why do they hate me? What did I do to them?"

"They don't fucking hate you. It was just something to say. Besides, there's been plenty of women up here."

"And how many of them have been working for you?"

He stepped further into my room and glared at me. "What the hell are you talking about?"

"I know exactly what you're doing up here. I know why I'm here too. You recruit people like me to work for you!"

Jake threw back his head and laughed. "So tell me something I don't know."

"You even asked Annemarie to take some smack back to Germany."

"Annemarie?" He acted as if he couldn't remember who she was.

"You know. Brigid and Annemarie. The two German girls in Chiang Mai."

"Yeah, so what? They could have made a lot of money." Then he pulled me over and wrapped his arms around my waist. "Nobody's asking you to do anything you don't want to do. All you've got to do is say 'no.'"

I was furious. My fingers curled into hard fists and I jumped on top of him and started pummeling him all over, but he didn't even flinch. Then he grabbed both my wrists and pushed me onto the mattress. "Stop acting crazy."

I felt the pressure of his arm release my head, and I was able to lift up my chin. "I've had enough," I gasped. "I'm getting out of here."

He threw his body on top of mine, burying his head in my neck, and letting out this long sorrowful moan. "Nooo. Don't fucking go."

"You mean you want me to stay so I can carry around more dope for you?"

He shook his head. "I never wanted you to get involved. You made that decision on your own. You're nothing like those other girls. You've got to trust me. You can leave anytime you want to."

It's not difficult to understand what happened next. It was not something I was forced into doing. There was no point where I had to make a decision "yes" or "no," just like a leaf doesn't decide to fall from a twig, or a bear to slink into a cave to hibernate. I became Cara's partner. Even though I knew Jake was using me, I thought I was using him too. I liked my life in northern Thailand. The money I made would allow me to stay in the country a little longer.

Our job was to hang around Chiang Mai looking for

customers: travelers who came north for drugs, or others who felt like indulging once they got there. We also delivered kilo packages when asked. Mostly, we sold small quantities of smack, but when someone needed something more, we knew where to get it. If we thought the *farangs* were junkies or wanted to bring the shit back home, we sent them over to a Chinese dealer. The guys up in Fang didn't want anything to do with addicts. Sooner or later junkies got busted and would do anything to protect their own skin, including give away their connections.

Both Cara and I acquired a bit of a habit too. Most times, we just snorted the stuff, sort of like drinking a cup of coffee in the morning to wake up, or taking a pinch in the evening to keep the good times rolling. After all, it wasn't easy to sit around bars all night and actually enjoy it. You wouldn't believe the jerks we had to talk to just to make a deal. Occasionally, when we were having a slow night, we'd quit early and go back to her room, where I'd watch her light a candle and take a singed spoon and syringe out of a small black velvet bag. Shooting up was her little secret. She saw it kind of like a tip, a gratuity, for all the work she was doing down there in Chiang Mai while the guys were up in Fang riding around on their dirt bikes, smoking opium in the motel, and drinking beer with their Thai partners. I was always a spectator, though, happy to get wasted, but never using a needle. I guess I still needed to feel as if I were in control and had a chance of salvaging some part of my life.

By then, blood was no longer the only vital force running through my veins. My moods and metabolism were controlled by the presence or absence of drugs. My body became polluted with caffeine, opiates, and whatever else I smoked or snorted.

On a typical day, Cara would still be asleep at three o'clock in the afternoon. She slept like a snake curled up and completely inert. The warmer the air, the better her slumber. I was never able to tell if she was breathing. Sometimes, it seemed as if nothing about her was moving, and I'd shake her awake because I was scared she might be dead. But with her eyes closed and body curled larvae-like under the sheets, I would stare at her and wonder how she ever became so hard. Physically, she didn't have an ounce of fat on her. Mentally, she pretended to be tough, as if nothing ever bothered her, but whenever we were high, she started rehashing moments in her life, like licking old wounds. After some attention, they wouldn't seem to hurt so much.

One night, when we were too high to get to sleep, she told me the story about the first time she tried to get off the streets. "When I was sixteen, I used to stand at the bus station behind Market Street with nowhere to go. I wanted to get up enough nerve to sneak onto one of those Greyhounds and ride up the coast to Portland or Seattle. People were getting off the buses and pouring through the gates, and I'd just be there like a rock in a rushing stream, while announcements came over the loudspeakers telling about the next bus to arrive or depart. Sometimes a cop would come over and ask me to show my ticket. When he saw I didn't have one, he'd tell me to move along. I fucking hated that. I had every right to stay in that bus station. I wasn't bothering anyone.

"One day, I decided to forget about getting to Eugene or Portland, or wherever the fuck I wanted to go at that moment, and just take a job downtown in the city. I didn't really want a job, but people had started giving us a hard time about panhandling. They say San Francisco is so liberal with all those gays and hippies living there, but don't believe it. They hated seeing kids begging on the streets. There were days I actually got spit on. I made them sick. And I began to think that maybe they were right. I wasn't retarded or anything. There really wasn't any reason I couldn't work, except why the hell would I want to? So I decided, fuck `em all. I *will* get a job. No job could be as hard as standing on Market hustling quarters from assholes.

"Some of my friends lied about their ages and tried working as cashiers in the Haight or as bike messengers downtown, but I must have been crazy to think that I could just walk into an office and get hired. When I started looking, I made sure I wore nice clothes. I had this wool skirt that came down to my ankles so no one could see my boots underneath. The counselor at the teen center picked out the skirt for me. I guess deciding to get a shitty job meant I was some kind of success story. She even persuaded me to lose my nose ring, but I left in my studs. It was only a job.

"I walked right into an office that was looking for someone to do filing. The building was old and dingy, kind of like the place you'd go to make a porno film. I had a few friends who did that. A woman from behind the counter handed me a clipboard with a pile of forms attached to it, and I sat down in a chair to fill them out. There were about twenty other ladies sitting around waiting too. They were older than me and had these large oval bodies and sagging cheeks. I don't think they even spoke English. They just sat there clutching their clipboards, looking scared and confused.

"The application was easy. Down at the center, I'd been practicing filling out forms. I even knew what post office box to write on the line that said 'address.' I wasn't exactly homeless, but I was living in a squat out on Harrison where we didn't get mail.

"When I was finished, I brought the clipboard back to the counter and the lady checked my work, as if I might have misspelled my own name. Then she put everything in a file and attached some more forms to the board. The first piece of paper was a job description, saying the company was looking for a file clerk, someone who could sort and file documents. I think the paragraph must have been some kind of disclaimer, because I had to sign a line at the bottom, stating I understood what the job was about and wouldn't fucking sue them when I wasn't made president of their goddamn company. Then I turned the page over and saw a form labeled Filing Test.

"A woman sitting next to me decided that it was lunchtime and took out some homemade tacos and started munching. Soon, the entire room smelled like a burrito stand. Shit, the meat smelled good. I hadn't eaten since the night before, but I tried to concentrate on what I was doing. The first part of the test had a list of different letters placed in rows, like a-b-g-c. The instructions said to cross out the letter that didn't belong in the sequence. The second part had a series of five letters, and I had to circle the letter that came before the others in the alphabet. Then there was a list of last names. I was supposed to put the names in alphabetical order. That's when I realized that the job I was applying for sure wasn't going to be any brain buster. Standing outside the bus station hustling coins was a thousand times more exciting than this shit. I sat in that office for a few more minutes thinking about the people at the teen center who were hoping I was going to turn over some  new leaf and join the real world, but then I bolted. I was back on Market within seconds."

*I*'m putting the pieces of Cara's life together. The more I learn, the less frightened I am of becoming like her. She's just one of these people who keeps on surviving, like a person who is constantly drowning, but comes bobbing back to the surface over and over, ready to take her last gulp of air.

The plan is that Cara and I deal in Chiang Mai, and every few weeks, go back up to Fang to get resupplied. We don't want to have a predictable routine where people know where to find us.

We each have our own little room in an old guesthouse across the river from Shangri-La. There aren't many tourists here, only those who have some place to go. I guess there are still people who take the word sightseeing seriously. In the daytime, the rooms are empty and a breeze blows through the stone stairway. The place is pretty gloomy, though. You just have to get used to it. There are all kinds of stains on the floors and walls: large yellow spills from beer or soda, dirty brown patches from mud and dirt, and rust-colored droplets of what might be blood. I don't want to look too closely, and the longer I'm here, the less I notice it at all. I'm happy to have a roof over my head and some place to sleep at night. If we move, change our routine, something bad will happen. I know it will.

When I was a kid, I had these two hamsters. They weren't very happy creatures. After all, they were stuck in a stinking cage all their lives. Inside the cage, they had their shavings, a *water bottle, a bowl of nuts and seeds, an exercise wheel, and a cardboard tube from a roll of toilet paper. Mom was always reminding me to clean out the cage, but the times the hamsters seemed to like their home the most was when there were nut shells, droppings, shaving scraps, and cardboard pieces all strewn around. That's when they were able to pile it all together and create a warm fluffy nest. But one day, Mom got so fed up with the smell that she thought she'd do me a favor and clean the cage herself. She dumped the carefully shorn bedding into the garbage and washed the base down with detergent, then presented the clean cage to me, probably hoping I'd feel guilty that I hadn't taken responsibility for those little rodents after spending so many weeks begging her to get them. The cage glistened and didn't even stink. The food bowl was filled with new nuts, the water bottle was scrubbed and shiny, but the change was too much. The hamsters died a few days later.*

On my next trip to Lek's, I set out for the bus station carrying my knapsack, passport, water, and  a few thousand baht. Cara was to meet me in Bangkok when I got there. A knot had tightened in my stomach, the way I began to feel every time I ventured away from my little room.

Thais were milling outside the gates of the terminal, but it was impossible to tell who was leaving and who was coming in. Everyone seemed to be camped under the hot sun for the duration. There were large families with lots of children and old people who looked as though they weren't going to live long enough to survive the journey back to their villages. There were also men and women squatting next to reed baskets where chickens flapped their wings like white feather flags of surrender. Babies cried. Barbecued pork sizzled on smokey grills. Vendors shouted. Dust scattered in clouds. And people pushed in great amoeba–like throngs toward the incoming buses.

If I was going to catch the next bus to Bangkok, I needed to find the gate, but all the signs were in Thai. It was hard enough to speak the language, but the script was impossible to read. Finally, I made my way over to where I was told the bus departed, but no bus was there. I figured it was being hosed down, filled with petrol, and presented to Buddha before making the long journey south, so I took a seat on the ground with the rest of the crowd. The only difference was that my knapsack contained a large envelope holding the brick of smack that would be cut many times over before it reached the States, then split into dime bags and sold on city streets in tiny glassine pouches with names like Death, Surrender, or White Night.

When a shiny first-class bus finally pulled up, we all clambered on. I kept my shoulder bag with me, but stowed the knapsack in the luggage compartment at the bottom of the bus like I thought we'd planned. If the bag wasn't in my possession, I was safe for at least a while. I felt better for about a second, until we were about to pull out and a Swiss man jumped on board. If we'd been in his country, or mine, there would have been little chance that he'd have chosen to sit next to me, but we weren't in Zurich or riding down the Pacific Coast Highway. I was another Western traveler, which meant we were like family, so he made himself comfortable and began talking. He was one of those people who had the ability to ask and answer his own questions. "So, you been to Chiang Mai? Where did you stay? Princess Guesthouse?"

I nodded. I didn't care I wasn't telling him the truth.

"You like Chiang Mai, yes? You go to hill-tribe village? Smoke opium with headman?" He laughed, imitating the classic tour guide line. "I go on trek once. Smoke so much opium, how do you say it? We were all off our heads. I see red and green dragons fucking for days."

I looked out the window at the succession of billboards written in English, German, French, and Japanese, announcing the mileage to the next umbrella factory. For a moment, I thought I could have been in the United States watching signs marking the distance to the next rest stop or scenic overlook, and he continued talking. "How long have you been in Thailand? Two, three weeks? I've been here for months. I love it, but it make me crazy. Do I act crazy? I was never like this before. Now I can't think. Don't want to think, you know."

His bloodshot eyes flashed at me, and I knew he was on speed. He probably sat next to me because he didn't want anyone suspecting that he was out of his mind, jabbering to an empty seat. Then he became quiet for a moment and peered at me. "You speak English, no?"

I smiled.

"Ja, ja. Everyone in Switzerland speaks English. It's good. Here, no one speaks German except a few Thais. They want to sell you something and they speak your language. Then you need something from them, and they don't fucking understand you."

"I don't speak German," I told him, hoping he'd stop talking.

"Good. Good. You going home? You want to buy drugs?"

I examined him closer, having heard about traps set by

DEA and Interpol agents, but I doubted any government organization could have masterminded a composite undercover like him. "I'm going to Bangkok. That's all," I told him.

He laughed. "That's all. How can that be *all*? Everyone takes home something from Thailand. What do you want? Heroin? Speed? Ecstasy?"

My stomach was cramping. Each word coming out of his mouth was hitting my bowels with a tonality that made me sink further into my seat. Instead of getting rid of him, I jumped up to find the toilet at the back of the bus, cursing that I stowed my knapsack in the luggage compartment when a bit of dope could have held my guts together for the rest of the trip.

When I returned, I reached for my water bottle, wishing Jake was with me. He'd have known how to get rid of the guy.

"What day is it," the Swiss asked suddenly. "Monday? Tuesday?"

"Thursday, I think."

He let out a rambling Germanic curse and pounded his fist against the seat in front of us. "Shit! I have date to pick up girlfriend at airport. I was supposed to be there yesterday." Then he reached into his pocket and pulled out a crumpled letter.

I smiled, glad this asshole wasn't a boyfriend of mine.

"Oh Christ," he blurted. "She's going to have my balls."

I needed that fool to move away from me quickly, otherwise my stomach was going to do something ugly. "Look," I whispered, "you seem like you need some sleep. Don't you have a pill or something?"

The Swiss stopped blabbering for a moment. His face

had become more flushed, but his eyes turned crafty, and he reached inside his shirt pocket and took out a small paper napkin which he quickly unwrapped. Inside were two capsules. "May I borrow your water?"

I handed him the bottle, only too happy to assist if it meant a few hours of peace. He threw the pills into his mouth and chased them down. Within minutes his eyelids closed, his head rocked against the back of the seat, and a string of saliva dribbled out of the corner of his mouth.

As the sun climbed higher into the sky, the passengers drew their dusty curtains across the windows to keep the inside of the bus cool. I started reading a glossy magazine about Hong Kong movie stars who had sex change operations, then dozed off. Sleeping had become such a comforting way of passing time. While my eyes were closed, the world still seemed unable to harm me.

When I woke up, the bus had pulled over in front of a gas station. The entire vehicle was empty, and the Swiss guy had disappeared. Outside the window, our luggage lay scattered across the dirt and two dogs were sniffing around each bag, as if they were looking for a good place to pee.

A group of soldiers guarded the periphery, eyeing the dogs carefully. The other Thai passengers were seated at long picnic tables, blissfully spooning rice and curried fish into their mouths. I prayed the dirty shirts and underwear inside my knapsack would hide all traces of the junk, but I didn't know how keen the dogs' sense of smell really was. I tried closing my eyes again, but every inch of my body tingled as if it were being continuously stunned by some invisible current. If the dogs picked out my knapsack, the soldiers would know it was mine. Without the Swiss on board, I was the only other Westerner there.

I sifted through alibis. I could say a friend gave it to me (that was true), and I had no idea what was in it (that was not). I could deny it was even mine. I could pretend I didn't speak a word of Thai. I practically didn't. The bag was lying in the dust. It smelled bad. I knew it did. All those days of sweat and dirt, the guesthouse floors, the strange luggage racks and baggage areas, had to amount to some hideous accumulated odor. How could a little parcel of dope have a scent at all, especially competing with the smell of coconut curry and gasoline in the air? If there were any sacrifices to make, I was ready to make them. Dysentery? I'd endure it. Asshole vets? Swiss guys on speed? Knowing what really bothers you is helpful when you're trying to barter for your life.

The other passengers stopped eating and began to mill about the piles of luggage. The dogs seemed to come to some very inconclusive findings and started rolling around on the ground, scratching their backs against the pebbles and dry earth. This did not make the soldiers happy. They quickly leashed them up and dragged them away, leaving the poor driver to throw the baggage back into the belly of the bus. I dashed off and threw up in the weeds, thanking Buddha, or whoever, and thinking that, if nothing else, I'd gotten rid of the Swiss guy for the rest of the trip.

Later that day, we arrived in Bangkok just as the sun was setting. I felt raw. Everyone seemed to be looking at me, as if by just having fair skin and light hair I was drawing attention to myself. I needed to be anonymous, among people who spoke my language and looked like me, so I headed for Khao San Road and the Siam Guesthouse.

Po recognized me right away. "You look different," he remarked. It probably wasn't the first time he saw the strange ways his country changed its travelers.

"Well, I'm the same," I assured him.

He winked. "Same same, but different. Where's your husband now?"

I almost forgot that Ben and I used to call each other "husband" and "wife." It was easier than explaining the complications of our relationship. "He's in Chiang Mai," I lied.

Po looked curious. "Now you here and he there? *Mei pen rai.* You not miss him, you see."

Well, he was right. When I first arrived in Bangkok, nothing would have convinced me that five months later, I'd end up alone in the very same room of the guesthouse where we first stayed. In all that time, how many other travelers had passed through that door? Yet there was no evidence of anyone else. The room was still barren with no furniture to collect dust. The WC in the courtyard had remained a watery swamp with a hose for a shower, and a deep ceramic pool and plastic bucket to dip into to flush the squat toilet.

A small mirror stood over the sink outside the bathroom door, and I looked into it, not fully recognizing the person who was staring back at me. My skin was tanned a rich brown, my face was angular and lean, and my tangled hair was streaked blond in a way I had never seen it. My eyes sparkled aqua, like the shimmering light off a swimming pool, even though on my driver's license, my eyes were listed as green. At first, I wondered how the change had happened so quickly, but then I realized that identity is a fluid concept, and enough time had passed for substantial transformation.

That night, I went down to the bar to visit Po who poured me free beers and talked about the psychology degree he was getting at Chulalongkorn University. I had no idea he even attended college. Whenever I saw him, he was cracking open beer bottles and strutting around to Donna Summer, using the neck of a Singha as an imaginary microphone. He told me he knew an English girl who just got a job talking to Japanese businessmen, and he thought I should look into it too.

"Just talking?" I asked.

"English conversation," he explained, his eyes twinkling.

"What else would I have to do?"

"Maybe drink some champagne, laugh a lot, make them feel like they're having good time."

I sighed. "That sounds too Thai."

"Five hundred baht an hour."

I took a sip of beer and felt the breeze from the ceiling fan brush against the top of my head. A couple of red-faced *farangs* wandered in from the street and peered inside, looking at us like we were wax sculptures. They whispered something to each other, then the man approached Po and asked the price of a room. Po told him, but the *farang* scowled. The rooms weren't expensive, especially for someone just coming in from the West, so I tried to ignore their charade. As they walked by, the girl leaned in my direction, wanting to know if the place was clean, as if Po wasn't standing right there and couldn't answer truthfully himself. I shook my head and pinched my nose, snickering as the couple took my advice and walked away.

When I went out on the street that night, the sight of all the vendors made me dizzy. I strolled along the sidewalk taking in the endless stalls of jewelry, tapes, books, and clothing. Everything seemed so abundant. Crowds of Westerners were trying on silver rings and bracelets, listening to CDs playing in the humid air, and chatting about the places they'd been. The notices hanging on the bulletin board at Sunni's Restaurant were still there: someone was selling a pair of hiking boots, another was looking for a one-way ticket to Hong Kong. There were signs posted over other signs—scores and scores of travelers communicating with one another—but nothing more about Cara. Her picture must have been covered over a long time ago.

Off in a corner, a girl kept staring at me as if I were some sort of apparition. I knew why she was looking at me that way, and I wanted to go over and put my hand on her shoulder, reassuring her that I was indeed alive. I was not some ghost, and she didn't have to worry. She wasn't looking into the mirror, and I'd never be the reflection she'd see. I understood her confusion, though. It was the initial terror of traveling into the unknown that made us all want to find quick answers about what was to become of us in the future, even if those answers were not so well conceived.

At the scheduled hour, I went to Soi Cowboy. The *tuk-tuk* driver drove like a maniac, swerving in and out of cars, kissing bumpers with other *tuk-tuks*, and dodging pedestrians and overloaded buses, as if he were playing a video game and he was going to score more points with each close call. Finally, he pulled a one-eighty where Soi Cowboy became a pedestrian walkway and grinned proudly at his maneuvers. I reached into my wallet to pay him and took out a one hundred baht bill. He deserved every bit of it, and I hoped he would speed away and out of my life forever.

By then it was late at night and Soi Cowboy was filled with Caucasians wearing floppy hats, baseball caps, designer T-shirts and Bermuda shorts. Their faces were red and splotchy from jet lag and too much sun, but they created the perfect camouflage for me, and I remember thinking that when the Martians come down from outer space to take back some specimens of Earthlings, they'll probably wonder why we are all divided into groups with names like Polo and Calvin Klein stenciled onto our shirts.

At Lek's, Cara greeted me as if she'd been waiting there for hours. Up at Fang, I'd overheard her argue with Mike about letting me carry the stuff alone, but Mike insisted it was safer that way. He said I needed the experience and a new face would keep suspicions away from her.

"Where's Lek?" I asked, as she grabbed the bag from my shoulder.

I slipped off my sandals and went into the apartment. Even though I didn't know Lek well, I felt that the first time I was there we'd made some kind of connection. Beneath his calm exterior, he seemed so unhappy about his whole existence. Somehow, I hoped he'd take the time to get to know me, but when I saw him again, I knew he was strung out.

"Umm," he murmured when he noticed me. He was leaning against a pile of pillows and strumming an electric guitar without an amp. I started to go over to him, but Cara was shouting something from the front room. By the time I reached her, she'd dumped all my clothing out on the floor. "Where the fuck is it?" She demanded.

"What do you mean?"

"It's not here. Someone's stolen it. Who the hell was with you?"

"I came here by myself."

"Well, did you talk to anyone or leave the bag any-where?"

I leaned against the wall. "It was in the luggage compartment all the way from Chiang Mai."

Cara gave me a hateful look. "The luggage compartment?"

"Isn't that what we said? If the bus was searched, I wouldn't have to claim it."

She groaned. "What are the chances of the bus being searched?"

"Don't you understand? It *was* searched. Dogs and everything. If they found the dope, I wouldn't be here now." In my mind, I went through the moments between when the bus was stopped and the baggage thrown onto the road. I'd been asleep, but that was also when the Swiss guy disappeared.

"Shit, shit, shit," Cara repeated.

"I was sitting with some idiot on speed. After the rest stop, he never came back."

"Why didn't he take your whole bag then? How could he have known what was in it?"

From the back room Lek groaned. "Concentrate," Cara ordered. "Think about everything you did."

"I was sick. I went to the toilet a lot."

"We're fucked. Someone's ripped you off."

I peered through the doorway to where Lek was biting his lip and strumming. In the background, I could hear the din from the crowds on the street below. Laughter roared up to us on the second floor, then subsided. The cry of the *farangs* must have reminded him of some business he need-ed to attend to. He pulled himself up, his head lilting to one side, his body following the same slant, and mumbled that he had someplace to go. Cara ignored him and kept pacing the floor, shooting questions at me. "Who pulled your bus over, the army or the police?"

"They were wearing uniforms. That's all I know."

"There was a dog?"

"There were two. They didn't smell a thing."

"Maybe there wasn't anything to smell. The police could have taken the package by then. They could be trailing us."

I rubbed my head feeling confused. "The police?"

Cara looked at me as if I was pitiful. "We're never going to get it back. The guys will kill me."

"But it's not your fault. I'll explain everything. Jake will understand."

I was one of the saddest cases she'd ever seen. "You're going to have to tell them. It's like thousands of fucking dollars. You don't know much about Jake, do you? Moving this shit is all he cares about."

We sat in that room talking about what could have happened until the dark sky outside turned light. Soon, there was a rattling at the door and Lek let himself in. He looked revived, as though he was returning from a morning's shopping, and hadn't been out hustling tourists half the night. "You bring more business for me," he giggled, as though he hadn't seen me just a few hours before.

"Someone's ripped Maddy off," Cara announced.

Lek frowned. "No worries. I get everything back."

I shook my head. "It had to have been the police."

Lek sat down and lit a cigarette. That was the first time I actually saw a Thai look worried. I'd seen police and security guards look mean, and old monks look solemn and distant, but Lek's frown scared me. "Maybe I have uncle who can help," he offered.

"Forget it," Cara muttered. "We're never going to get it back."

"I'll do anything," I begged.

"I'm going out for a while," she announced. "I have to clear this shit up."

Once Cara left, Lek brought me over a glass of water and began massaging my neck, his fingers digging deep into my muscles, nearly making me cry out in pain. "You very sad girl," he whispered. "You no belong here. Why not get on plane and go home?"

Tears began to fill my eyes. The mixture of kind words and brutal acts upset me. "Maybe I should. I don't know what to do anymore."

"Why you stay here? Why you not go home?"

"I love Thailand."

He made a face and opened his arms wide. "This is not Thailand. This is ugly place. It is slum."

He continued rubbing my shoulders, and I felt my skin become hot and damp. "Well, you live here."

He shook his head. "I live here because no have choice. If I rich *farang*, I get away too. What about family? You not have mother or father who miss you? Or sisters and brothers, aunties and uncles?"

"It's not like that over there," I said weakly. "We're all alone. It's everyone for himself. No one cares about relatives or what you'd think was important."

Lek made a face as if he didn't understand.

"America isn't like Thailand," I continued. "In the U.S., children grow up and move away from their parents, not take on more responsibility for them. Besides, what about

Cara? I can't leave her now. Look what I've done."

"Cara can take care of herself."

"She'll be angry if I go."

"Cara will be Cara. She was Cara before she met you."

I thought about that a little longer, wishing I were somewhere else, maybe up in the mountains swimming under the cool waterfall or sitting quietly beneath the leaves in that little grotto where the reclining Buddha lay. Lek was right. There were so many truly beautiful spots in Thailand. Why had I chosen to spend my time the way I did? "I should go back to Fang and tell them I quit. If I stay, I'll ruin everything."

He led me over to a mat and lay me down. "You need to rest. You must be strong."

Blood rushed to my head as he sat on his knees next to me and started massaging my scalp, each fingertip pressing into my skull, touching places that made my whole body tingle. But when I looked up, I saw the purple punctures in his skin—track marks running up and down the insides of his arm—and knew he was tied to something just as meaningless as I was.

It was late afternoon when I woke up. Lek was gone. Heat filled the room and minute particles of dust danced in the sunlight. I wanted to get out of there before anyone returned, but leaving wasn't easy. I'd been sick for weeks and didn't have much energy. With enough anesthetic you can hide a lot of pain. I craved simplicity. I needed to be a tourist again, to gape at the golden mosaics on temple walls or watch the long-tailed boats zigzag back and forth across the Chao Praya River.

Downstairs, I caught a *tuk-tuk* and sat back as we raced toward my destination, the Royal Palace. I felt safe there. I'd visited it many times when Ben and I first arrived. Inside the gates, there was no racing traffic, mad drivers, or touts calling out about one more sex bar. In the compound, the air was still and serene. The buildings were lined with gleaming sculptures, figurines from the Ramakien: Hanuman the monkey god, and jeweled warriors holding up the palace walls. Along the neat paths, novice monks shuffled by, discreetly turning sideways to catch one more look at me, the Westerner, as I walked past. I stared at them too. Most were only fifteen-or sixteen-year old boys giving up one year to Buddha and the next to the Thai army. They didn't seem to mind their sacrifice. I'd seen schools of them traveling around Bangkok before, orange fish, on their way to different temples or shrines while listening to soccer scores on their transistor radios.

Once, during a sudden thunderstorm, Ben and I ended up huddled in a stone doorway with a seventeen-year old monk. He was as curious about us as we were about him. After trying some hand signals, he wrote the name and address of the *Wat* where he was staying and told us to come by after eleven o'clock that night when the other monks started to really party. There was going to be whiskey, beer, and all kinds of drugs, but we never went. Back then, I'd been disappointed at his lack of piety.

A slate path led deep into the palace grounds, and I came to a long rectangular building, Wat Pha Keo. Inside, there was one large room where the Emerald Buddha sat high on a raised altar. No chairs or mats were in the chamber, but the room was cool, and visitors could stay sitting on the floor undisturbed for hours. I slipped down onto the tiles, staring at the sculpture that looked so smooth and strong. I wanted to absorb the power emanating from the stone, feel its peacefulness, and know I had the strength to overcome whatever was debilitating me. It was in that cool temple that I think I first understood the power of religion and how one figure, real or imagined, could truly help someone struggle through difficult times.

K R A P P Y      G U E S T H O U S E
F A N G
J U N E

*L* ate afternoon inside my green pepper room. Where the hell is Jake? They're probably up in the hills watching the crop grow. No, men with machine guns do that. I've seen them in their mirrored sunglasses, blue jeans, and side arms, riding around in the back of pickups. They scare me. I can't tell who works for who. Do the guys use the Thais to farm the poppies, or do the Thais need the Americans to get the stuff out of the country? It doesn't matter. I'm not going to be here much longer. Cara can stay forever. What can they do to me? I'm not a prisoner here. There's this internal clock ticking fast inside me telling me to leave. I listen to my body. Women have experience doing that. Menstruation gives us faith to trust the signs inside ourselves. Then there's ovulation, PMS, or the moment when the erogenous zones click into desire. Usually, the body reacts before the mind has time to process that reaction, then the cerebral catches up. That's what I'm doing now. Catching up. My body's kept a secret from my consciousness for a long time, but now I know it's time to go.

On my way up to Fang, I stopped in Chiang Mai and took a *songthaew* across the canal to Shangri-La. As usual, the sun blazed hot and yellow in the sky. Sitting across from me was a Scandinavian couple who just arrived. They looked around anxiously as if they were lambs being taken to slaughter. I laughed to myself, wanting to tell them that when it happens, it won't be like this. You'll never know when you're going to end up over your head, and when you do, you'll be a willing participant, and it'll be too late. That's just the Thai way.

It was early, and I figured Juliette would be asleep, so I didn't mind waiting outside her door after I knocked. When she finally appeared, she looked awful. Her face was pale and her eyes were sunken and dark. She reminded me of the way Pascal had looked right before he died.

"Juliette?"

"*Oui*," she blinked uneasily.

"It's me. Maddy."

"Maddy?" She opened the door wider, and I could smell the sour odor of medicines and unwashed sheets. Inside, the room was completely dark. I didn't want to go in, just in case she'd caught some kind of contagious disease, but she assured me I didn't have to worry.

"Aren't you working today?"

"I do not work any longer. Look at me."

I did look at her. She was wearing a man's T-shirt, which hung below her knees. On the backs of her calves were coin-sized welts.

"Can I leave the door open? You should get some air."

"Just a little. I do not want anyone to see me like this."

"But what's wrong with you?"

"It's nothing. I just need to rest."

"You're so thin. You've lost so much weight."

She pulled herself up and went over to the bedside table where she slid a cigarette out of an open pack. "To tell you the truth, I really can't eat much anymore."

"Have you seen a doctor?"

She exhaled from the corner of her mouth and looked annoyed. "No doctor will want to see this. I know. There's nothing to be done."

"Don't you think you should tell someone?"

She shook her head. "It's too late. Now I must sit and wait. My body aches all over. I feel like I've been hit by so many trucks. I'd really like to smoke some ganja. Do you know where I could get some?"

I smiled, thinking she'd picked the right person to ask. I knew where to get enough weed to supply all the *farangs* in Chiang Mai.

She reached for her wallet, but I pushed her money away.

"Would you mind going downstairs and bringing me some water too?"

I looked around the room, hoping I could spot whatever else she needed, but there were so many half empty containers and vials, I couldn't tell what any of them were. "Remember when I was sick in the room next door?"

"I don't think it is the same," she said softly.

"No. But you looked after me. I felt better just knowing you were there and knew how bad I was feeling."

She shrugged. "It is okay. What else could I do?"

I didn't want to explain to her that at the time she'd been the only friend I had. Now I was afraid that I was the only one who cared about her.

The groceries were easy to find. I picked up everything from a little shop nearby. When I returned, she was fully dressed and sitting outside her room. She'd set up two chairs so we could look out into the garden below. Her sleeveless dress exposed her bony shoulders, but if I hadn't looked too closely I never would have guessed how sick she really was.

She sucked on a joint as if it were a cigarette, never once passing it over to me. "That's better," she sighed, stretching her legs out in front of her and pointing her toes. "I used to be a dancer, *tu sais*?"

I nodded, thinking I'd heard the story before.

"No. A *dancer*," she repeated, doing a little jeté with her right foot. "I studied since I was four. Ballet. Modern. Tap. Jazz. *Toutes*. Before school, after school, I trained. When I was sixteen, I had the body of a twelve-year old boy. Everyone wanted me to go on to dance with the Ballet Français or some such." She went through the different arm positions as she spoke: first, second, third, fourth. "I joined a company for a while, but then I got fed up. I was so young and was never having any fun. It was always work, work, work. Finally, I quit and went to Amsterdam."

"Did you dance there?"

"Of course. I did my best dancing there. That's how I made enough money to travel. Once I started, it was always easy to find work." By the way she shook her hips, I knew what kind of work she meant.

The heat of the morning was building, and suddenly it felt as if all the turbulence in the atmosphere seized up. The flies no longer buzzed, the birds stopped chirping, the palm fronds didn't rustle, and we stopped talking. Although the balcony above kept us in shade, I was sweating. "Are you thirsty?" I asked.

Juliette ran her tongue across her cracked lips. "I would love *un jus d'orange*. I've been drinking only water for so many days."

"Hasn't anyone been taking care of you?"

"No one knows."

"What about the people at the club?"

"What do they care? I'll ruin business if I show up there. Look at me; I'm half dead already."

Juliette's face was ashen. The white of her sundress and the pallor of her skin made her seem like a phantom.

"What about that Thai you were with?"

"Thais don't understand illness. For them, it's more than a physical thing."

"Maybe I can find a European doctor?"

"They wouldn't know what to do. There is no cure, you know."

The heat clamped down on my head, tightening its grip. How was it possible that someone so young was convinced she would never recover? Was medicine really that lame, that in an age where organs were transplanted and cancers beaten, nothing could be done to help her?

"I think I'd better go inside," she whispered, pushing herself out of the chair. "The sun is very strong and I feel so tired."

I followed her back into the room and cut open a carton of orange drink to pour into a glass. "Have you thought about going home?"

She nodded and took some time to speak. "I want to go home. *Vraiment*, but it's too much trouble. I don't even know where my passport is. I haven't money for the plane ticket, and now that I've stopped working, how will I ever get any?"

"Can't you call your parents? Won't they send you some?"

She smiled weakly. "My parents? But I haven't spoken to them in months. You remember Pascal? When his parents came to get his body, they told me that when he left Belgium they never expected him to return alive."

"Then why did they let him go?"

Juliette shrugged. "The Belge are like the French, they like certainties, like Sunday dinners and August vacations. It was as if all along they wished him dead just so they could know where he was."

"What was wrong with him?"

Juliette gazed down at her hands; her eyelids looked blue like faint early morning light. "It was SIDA, like me."

Even though I knew I couldn't catch it just by being near her, I tried not to breathe. She must have sensed this and shook her head. "You cannot get it from me. I caught it at the club. Mr. Tam never said 'no' to customers, but he was always replacing girls who you'd never see again. Now I'm one of those girls."

"Shh," I told her, rubbing my fingers across the translucent skin on the top of her hand.

My touch seemed to relax her, and I used the time to glance around the room for an address book, a diary, anything that might have her parents' telephone number in it. Her family needed to be contacted. I would have called the French consulate myself, except I was worried about the questions I'd be asked. All I knew was that I had to take care of her. I wasn't going to let her suffer alone, but I had to finish a few things in Fang first.

When the motorbikes finally pulled in, the guys made a lot of noise as they usually did whenever they came back drunk from a bar or restaurant. Of course, they were talking about women. When they weren't talking about drugs, most of their conversations revolved around the benefits of Thai girls versus Western women. Mike had even been married to a Thai once, but it didn't last. The girl thought he was going to take her back to the States. That was the last thing on his mind. Besides the housekeeping and free sex, she was his excuse to stay up in the mountains without arousing too many suspicions.

Jake must have seen the light in my room because he poked his head through the door. His jeans and T-shirt were covered with yellow dust from the road. "Everything go okay?"

I was silent. I'd been rehearsing that moment for several days. My journal was out, and I kept scribbling in it to avoid looking at him.

"Aren't you going to put that thing down and say hello?"

"Hello," I replied. Even from a few feet away, I could smell the alcohol on his breath. I didn't want to get into a serious discussion with him if he was drunk. It was when he was drunk and I was sober that we had our worst arguments.

"What's so important that you have to write it in *there*?" he wanted to know, his voice rising. "Do you mind putting that goddamn notebook away. You've been gone for days. What the hell's going on?" Then he swiped the journal from my hands and flipped through the pages, reading it out loud, mocking each word I'd written there. When he looked up, his eyes were black. "Are you crazy? Why are you taking notes like this?"

"They're not notes."

"Jesus Christ. You've practically documented everything we do up here."

The diary always seemed a safe way to try to understand what was happening to me. I never thought anyone would read it or might use it as evidence against him as he was implying.

"You knew I kept a journal."

"I didn't know it was something that could get us all fried."

His breathing slowed and he seemed to relax. I didn't want to upset him, and I thought I knew how I could calm him down. When I put my arms around him, his body slackened. Even *he* couldn't help responding to affection, and he let me hug him. I took his hand and led him back to the bed, then reached over to unzip his jeans. He liked it when I went down on him and worked his prick with my tongue and lips while he lay back and puffed on a cigarette. I could always tell when he got into it because he'd put the cigarette aside, close his eyes, and recline against the pillows. When it was over, he'd pick up the cigarette again and take a long drag. Usually, it was still lit, and I had to be careful that the ashes didn't fall on me.

Later, I sat there with my head under his arm feeling sweaty and rancid, listening to the ceiling fan cut through the air. I'd gotten over the hardest part. He was no longer angry, but I felt a new kind of emptiness. I didn't hate him, but I certainly didn't love him either and that made me sad.

"How far would you go?" he asked, pulling me up closer and reaching his hand under my shirt.

"Sexually?"

"I've seen people do crazy things to survive. We're just animals, you know, if you really think about it. When you lose your will to survive, you'll be killed or eaten alive."

I listened, silently wondering if this was another lesson

from the war. They all had their little war riffs they could segue into if you pushed the right buttons. Pete went on about "the Asian mind," and cruelty. Mike talked about conspiracies and being abandoned by his country. With Jake, it was always the psychological stuff. Living with them had made me wonder what other soldiers who returned to civilian life were carrying around inside them.

"I can do what it takes," I told him, thinking about the blow job I'd just given.

"I'm not talking about giving good head. I mean, could you harm someone else to save your own life?"

"I guess I'll have to wait and see."

His eyes narrowed on mine. "I can, and that's what protects me better than any firearm."

"Maybe you can protect me while you're at it," I laughed.

"Look at you," he continued, pulling away and pointing to my diary. "What the hell are you doing? Who the fuck is this Juliette and why do you think she needs you so much?"

"She's sick. She's got AIDS."

"She's a whore."

"She was an exotic dancer."

"If she's French and she's doing fuck shows in Thailand, then she's a whore. How else do you think she got sick?"

I took a deep breath, not wanting to let him hear my voice tremble. "Juliette is a friend of mine. She might be the only one who cares about me here. If worrying about a friend is a sign of weakness, then I must be pathetic. Why don't you just admit it? You guys live up here where everything's under your control. No one knows you're here.

There are no new people. Nothing unexpected will ever happen. You don't want to feel anything, and being with me makes you remember that you have feelings, and that scares the shit out of you."

Jake stood up and threw his cigarette out the screen door, then turned back to me. "You're fucking right, but this is how I choose to live. It's how I want to be."

"Don't make me feel sorry for you with that war bullshit. The war was over twenty years ago."

Jake's eyes caught on fire. I'd crossed the line, but I had one more thing to tell him. "Someone stole that kilo I was supposed to bring to Lek." Then, I jumped off the bed and ran out into the night.

Outside, the air was cool and quiet. The cream-colored stars twinkled in the rich black sky. A crescent moon cast shadows on the road, where a dog lay like a flat tire, bloated, belly to the ground. I heard Jake kick open the screen door. His footsteps came crunching behind me.

Just like Cara, he made me go over every little detail of what had happened. "It must have been the police," he guessed. "Someone's screwing us over."

"I feel so awful. I'm so useless. I made everything go wrong."

He sighed and seemed to calm down. "It could have happened to any one of us: you, me, Cara. We've got to straighten it out. Nothing terrible's happened yet."

I could smell the cigarette smoke coming from the room next door. I knew that Mike and Pete were inside, but against the hum and sputter of the air-conditioning, they probably hadn't heard a word we'd said. Jake left me, and I sat down in a broken lawn chair just inside the gate. From outside the fence, a hibiscus bush stretched its long branches through the wire and brushed against my cheek, offering its closed blossoms to me. I held the furled flowers in my hand and touched the rough chiffon petals, wishing I could just curl up and disappear.

Jake didn't come into my room that night, although I waited for him there. The next morning, I heard a lot of movement and knew the guys were leaving. When Jake appeared at my door, I let him in without a problem, thinking it was probably the last time we'd be together. He lay down on the green bedspread and lit a cigarette while I sat at the edge of the mattress. The heat was just beginning to mount, and a dull hum seemed to fill the air. There was so much I wanted to tell him, about us, about me, but some alternate plan seemed to have been set in motion.

"I guess I'll see you down at Chiang Mai," he said solemnly. "I'm going to Bangkok for a couple of days."

I took a cigarette from his pack. "Yeah. A couple of days."

"You should get away from here too."

I nodded.

"Are you going back to Chiang Mai?"

I kept silent.

"What's the matter. You don't want to tell me?"

"I'm not making any plans," I explained, stretching myself out on top of him. His stomach muscles tightened against my ribs, and I twisted my toes around his feet, locking myself to him one last time. He wrapped his arms around me, and in one swift move, swept me underneath him.

That was the last time we made love. Neither of us ever said anything. I knew it was the end, though. And by the way he held me, he must have known too.

Less than an hour later, his motorbike started up and I watched from the screen door as he sped away. Then Mike was there. "How long you planning on hiding in here? Everything's gonna be taken care of. You just gotta be discreet."

"I wish it never happened. I just want to forget."

"Mrs. Chang's going to make dinner tonight. Why don't you come and eat with us?"

I agreed, although I wasn't looking forward to sitting down with Mrs. Chang while she spat words of advice. On the other hand, she was a great cook and I hadn't eaten a good meal in days. Maybe with Mike and Pete eating too, her attention wouldn't be so focused on me. Deep down she had a good heart. I guess I was hard on her because I thought she always had her nose in my business. It was partially my fault, though. I'd let her wash my clothes and leave meals for me, and in return she wanted company, but even that kind of commitment was hard for me to make.

That night, we ate ginger chicken with rice and Chinese cabbage; a change from the usual pad thai or soupy curries I bought from vendors on the street. During dinner, Mrs. Chang didn't sit down, but shuffled around, bringing us food, swatting at flies, and pouring jasmine tea out of a clay pot. She was one of those people who thought that if her guests weren't constantly eating, the meal was a failure, and since we couldn't eat and talk at the same time, she rambled on for us.

"You hear about old Tai up in the hills, ah? His daughter only fourteen. She work down in Bangkok. He says she get job cleaning office building. I tell him in Bangkok, no have jobs like that for young girls. Girls there are for one thing only. If you send daughter to Bangkok, you send her to be whore, that's all. Isn't that correct, Mike?"

I watched Mike dip his chopsticks into the rice and pull out a piece of chicken. "There's nothing wrong with being a whore, Mrs. Chang," Mike teased. "Thai girls make great whores."

Mrs. Chang agreed. "Sometimes Thai people don't say what they mean. Chinese people say everything what's on their mind."

I laughed nervously, but my enthusiasm turned Mrs. Chang's scrutiny back to me. "Americans don't tell truth either. Not like Chinese girl. American girl pretend to be so good. But Maddy, why you no like Thai boys? You come all this way and all you do is sleep with American men."

I kept quiet and pretended to pick a grain of rice from between my teeth.

"You no fool me. When you first come here, I think, oh, you little lost girl. Just like I see these men and think they old, but they act like teenager boys."

I caught Mike and Pete staring into their rice bowls.

"Was your daughter a good girl?" I asked quickly.

Mrs. Chang stopped whisking stray bits of rice off the table. I imagined the flocks of mynas that would descend on the grass at dawn waking me with all their chatter.

"Seow Lin was good girl. I taught her. She went off with American, but that okay. She only seventeen. Her father say no, but me, I think it good idea. American will take her to his country and they make money. Here, she only Chinese. No good. Say Maddy, why you no write home? Why no one worry about you? I hear about American girls. They come and go. They no care about anything, only themselves. Why you no want to get married? Why you no want children?"

"I'm only twenty-five."

Mrs. Chang shrugged. "So what. You body able."

Mike raised his eyes just far enough to make contact with mine. He knew how I felt about getting grilled by Mrs. Chang. "Mrs. Chang," he asked, "what would happen if all American girls had babies? Think about all the American babies there'd be running around the earth."

Mrs. Chang stuck out her lower lip. "Maybe you right. America is number one, but we don't need so many American babies."

I left the table soon after that. Mike and Pete stayed and drank another beer that Mrs. Chang eagerly poured into their glasses.

The next day, I packed my bags. There was nothing left on the carpet, only my lumpy knapsack full of ragged clothing and crumbling books. I guess there is something to be said about smacking cotton shirts against stones every time they are washed. Each T-shirt and dress had become a limp piece of cloth, not nearly measuring up to the type of garment it used to be, but my bag had become light and easier to carry.

I settled up with Mrs. Chang. When I first arrived, I paid her every few days, then every week or two, until finally the last bill came to 150 dollars—an entire month's total. I was down to my last 200 dollars again, with no prospect of making any more, but this time I wasn't worried. I knew I could survive. I only needed one meal a day, and a plate of rice and chicken from a stand on the street only cost about fifteen cents. If I had to, I would get a job just like Juliette had. By then I was certain that no matter where I went, there was always going to be a bar waiting to hire someone like me.

Pete and Mike had left earlier that morning. I felt relieved when I heard their motorcycles pull away. Their departure was routine, no checkout or other formalities. Mrs. Chang slipped into their rooms and clucked her tongue in astonishment as she gazed at the wreckage she was going to have to clean up. Clothes were strewn all over the floor and half-empty beer bottles sat in every corner. "They think I their mother," she complained. I didn't want to tell her that I didn't know any American mom who would stand for such a mess.

Then, like a snail who carries her home on her shoulders, I hoisted my knapsack on my back and left Mrs. Chang's for good. She seemed sad to see me go and told me that even in my rags, I was still the prettiest guest she ever had. Somehow, I must have reassured her that her hotel still had a bit of class.

*J*uliette is not getting better. If I wait for her to improve, I'll never leave Chiang Mai. Sometimes, I sit in her stuffy room with no air circulating and wonder how long it will take. Days? Weeks? Months? I don't want her to die, but maybe it's just easier that way. I've never really been this close to death. Now I see how inevitable it is. Just one more transition the body must make.

Each day, I bring her a cup of noodle soup, the kind that's sold in the States and only takes three minutes to make, but she can't eat the noodles until she's smoked some dope. Opium makes her feel better. After a bowl or two, the food slides easily down her throat. Some days she tells me she feels weak, and I have to hold her head and feed her like a baby. Usually, though, she can take care of herself. I don't think she's ever had to rely on anyone as much as she relies on me, and she doesn't like it much. Today, I left her in bed while I went out to buy some water. When I returned, she'd gotten herself dressed and was sitting downstairs at the picnic table smoking cigarettes and laughing with the other guests. I didn't want to say anything to her about conserving her energy and not ruining whatever health she has left. I have to let her live her own life.

A few days ago, she wanted help writing a letter. What we wrote made me cry.

Cher Maman et Papa:

You've always been so rational and taught me that good and bad things happen for a reason. If I fell and scraped my knee, it was because I was clumsy and had tripped on an uneven paving stone. If I laughed, it was because I was being tickled by someone's fingers, or a friend had told a funny joke. When I was younger I believed you, and your words gave me the confidence to continue dancing, as if every child could become a ballerina like I had. When I had enough and quit ballet, I know you were disappointed. I thought I could go away and pursue whatever gave me pleasure and make you proud of me again, but soon I was far from home and I learned that I was not so special.

I got myself into situations that you, in your bourgeois apartment in Paris, will never understand. But all through this, I've discovered things I can believe in. The Thais think that when you are born, a map of your life has already been set out for you, and I've met Americans who believe you can always change your destiny, but my experience tells me that neither is true. There is only luck; good luck and bad luck. The choices you make may lead you to one or the other, and I am here at the other. I've had bad luck, and there is no choice I can ever make that will change this. If there is good luck, it is that you will arrange to take me back to France. I know I haven't written in many months, and I can't even promise anything in return. I am very sick and need your help. Please, come and take me home.

Your Daughter,

Juliette

When she finished dictating, she sat back, broke off a piece of opium, and put it in her pipe. It wasn't a good day. She looked pale and her eyes were red and swollen. Then she asked for her tarot cards, something she's started doing regularly. Holding the deck in the palm of her hand, she waited until the opium took effect. Then, one by one, she lay out the cards on the bed in three long rows. Cards with little yellow stars twinkled against a rich black background. She told me they were pentacles and represented the physical being. There were other cards too: one with the picture of a gray tower crumbling to the ground; another of a woman seated at the gates of a temple, a veil covering her eyes, a book in her hand, and a serene expression on her face. Finally, there was a card with a picture of a man dressed in black, feet tied with a rope. He was hanging upside down from a branch of a tree. To me, it looked like the card of death, but she laughed. "It is not as terrible as that. It's the questions you ask that these cards can answer. For example, this hanging man doesn't mean everything is bad. Just look at his face. It is so calm. Maybe I have asked when I am going to France? This card tells me I must wait." She folded her cards back into the deck and looked at me closely. "Would you like me to read yours? They're only possibilities, you know. Nothing is certain."

"Whatever is in my future, I don't want to know," I told her.

But she urged me to choose ten cards from the deck, and I did, turning them over one by one and placing them in three rows, my eyes locking onto each one as if it could tell my destiny. Wands came up for me.

"You are adjusting the way you are around others," she began. "The way you see yourself and how you want others to see you. You may be feeling vulnerable or in doubt." Then she tapped the five of cups. "There are old feelings or relationships that are unresolved. You are trying to heal or protect someone, but you may be draining your energy by taking care of another."

"Are you talking about yourself?"

She frowned. "It is not me. It's the cards talking. It won't work if you don't believe." Then she leaned back against the cinder block wall. I didn't know what she was going to say next or if the reading was over, but I could tell that her mind had entered some region midway between consciousness and unconsciousness; a safe chamber where she could escape to with a little help from the dope.

C ara's back. I saw her at the AA Sports Bar. I couldn't avoid her even if I wanted to. Instead, we sort of trickled away from the different groups we were with and met at a neutral corner in the back of the room.

She acted normal, not angry or spiteful. When she asked about Fang, I told her about Jake.

"Does that mean you two are over?"

"Whatever there was, I guess."

"Too bad. I think he was really into you. I've never seen him act like that with another woman." Then she thought a minute and added, "Well, he used to be kinda like that with me."

I know she likes to tease me by making me believe she knows more about something than I do, and if she was trying to make me jealous, it worked. I always suspected she had some kind of relationship with Jake. They were just too friendly to be simply partners.

"Don't worry," she laughed. "It didn't work out."

A burst of reggae came over the loudspeakers. It was Bob Marley's Kaya, which is played everywhere like some sort of traveler's anthem album.

"What about money?" Cara asked. "You could work with me a while longer. I'm sure Jake won't mind."

I know Jake or Mike put her up to it just so she could

*watch over me. She doesn't want my company. Maybe she needs someone to boss around for a while. I won't help her much, other than by possibly protecting her from the onslaught of freaks and ravers who generate most of her business. Their steady stream will bring cash into my pocket. Then when Juliette goes home, I'll leave too.*

What happened next is difficult to describe. One day, on my way back to Shangri-La, I stopped at Lilly's Guesthouse. It had become a habit of mine—sort of a sick hope, or dread—that I'd bump into Ben there. I wanted to see how he had changed; like I knew I'd changed, in the way one wants to see an old childhood friend, just to confirm that there was a time when you both experienced the same things.

The courtyard and garden café were empty, and once again the place had been redecorated. This time the walls near the reception desk were covered with government posters written in English, advertising traditional Thai dinner dances and sound-and-light shows. I'd read about the new push to draw attention away from drugs and prostitution by offering tourists a dose of cultural fun instead. The evidence was all around me.

But the guesthouse hadn't been cleaned up completely. A string of airmail letters still hung off to one side; miniature flags flying foreign postal stripes. I stared at the envelopes, wishing one was for me. No one knew my address, but for a second I wanted someone to have missed me so much that they'd tracked me down and sent an aerogram filled with news from home. It wasn't likely though, and it was all my fault. I'd made little effort to correspond with anyone, so how could I expect them to even know I was there?

The letters came from faraway places like Germany, Sweden, France, and Canada; nothing from the United States. But just as I was about to walk away, a brown envelope without an airmail stamp or foreign insignia, caught my eye. It'd been mailed locally, and on it there seemed to be the same configuration of letters that made up my name. I examined it closer, still not believing that if you truly wanted something so badly, you could actually make it happen. But it *was* my name. I ripped the envelope down and tore it open, confident the letter was from Ben who'd tell me about some spiritual journey he was caught up in and how sorry he was that he hadn't come back to me. But there was only a tiny piece of lined paper inside, the kind children use for lessons in school, and it was signed by Eric.

My first thought was that he was writing in code. He said to send his winter parka. If he didn't receive his coat soon, he was going to freeze to death. Then the letter turned pitiful. He wanted to know why I never came to visit anymore and why he couldn't trust me.

Annemarie had told me he'd been transferred to some fancy American prison that I imagined was somewhere in the cornfields of Indiana. Why was he still behind bars in Chiang Mai? It made me sick to think how Jake and I had screwed him over by guiltlessly smoking what he thought of as his only hope of getting out. I stuffed the letter into the pocket of my knapsack, lifted the bag onto my shoulders, and made my way to Shangri-La.

Once I started working with Cara, I didn't deny myself much. Dope coated the world in a malleable ooze that was hard to extract myself from, and truthfully, I didn't even try. Some days, the elements of life dissolved into only a few certainties: we needed to get high, we got high, or we were coming down from being high.

"I think I remember you," Juliette told Cara one day when we were all sitting around Shangri-La waiting for the temperature to cool down so we could go out again. "Have you ever been to the prison?"

Cara was weighing out small quantities of H on an old-fashioned balance scale. She lifted her head from the weights and smirked as if she always knew one day this question would come up. "The guy I came to Thailand with is there."

I dropped the bag she had passed to me to seal. "Who are you talking about?"

From her mocking smile, I could tell she knew she was about to say something that would change our minds about her forever. Still, her eyes remained stuck on mine, even though Juliette was the one who'd asked her the question. "I came here with Eric."

Juliette glanced at me, and I tried to keep my expression steady. Relationships and betrayals crisscrossed through my head until Cara's image—the girl whizzing through Chiang Mai on the back of a motorbike; the girl visiting the prison with the hummingbird tattoo–settled there.

"But how did it happen?" Juliette wanted to know. "Why is he in prison?"

Cara waved something away, as if a fly were buzzing too close to her ear. "I don't give a shit anymore."

"Come on," Juliette urged. "You must tell."

Cara looked sideways, wanting to check if I was still listening, and of course I was. I'd practically put the whole story together before she even started.

"All right," she gave in. "It all started back in San Francisco when I first hooked up with my real dad. He owned this recording studio. My mom had gone all straight, but Dad hadn't changed since the seventies. We became friends. Sometimes I'd drop by his studio just to say hello and smoke some weed. Then he started inviting me up to his weekend house in Mendocino County. He even let me stay there when he wasn't around, but I was never alone. He had this girlfriend named Annie, who lived up there too. Annie was closer to my age than his. She was one of those southern California chicks who acted so innocent, but at the same time got away with doing almost anything. She slept all day, drank gallons of coffee, and sunbathed nude in the back garden, listening to Kate Bush on speakers she turned out the windows to face the redwoods. She liked my dad, but when he wasn't there she could forget about him too.

"She wanted to be an actress, but she never would have made it in Hollywood. She said she wasn't vulgar enough. She didn't like to give 'bjs.' That's what she called them.

"I told her I was lucky `cause I didn't have any ambition, but she didn't believe me. She kept on insisting that there had to be *something* I was good at.

"But when I thought about it, there really wasn't. I was doing much better than at any other time in my life. When I was with my mom and Don, I just wanted to get the hell out of their house. Then when I was on the streets, I couldn't think about much except where I was going to crash, who had the best weed, and what I had to do to get it. It felt fucking weird to be sitting in my own father's house with birds chirping all around, thinking there could be something more I might want.

"Most afternoons, Annie and I would drive into town to the Olde Tyme Tavern where tables were set up out on the sidewalk. Annie loved to drive my dad's Dodge Dart. She'd steer it out to the end of the driveway, then turn off the ignition, put the gears in neutral, and let it coast all the way down the hill. Her goal was to glide to the crossroads in the middle of town without touching the brakes or starting the engine again. Sometimes, she drove with her eyes closed, navigating by memory around the bends and curves, and I wondered how many more minutes we were going to be alive.

"One day, we were sitting outside the tavern drinking lemonade mixed with vodka we'd bought from the liquor store next door, when these two guys walked by in their splattered coveralls and baseball caps. They must have looked sexy to her, because she nudged me and called them over.

"They sat down and ordered Cokes, keeping their eyes on her sunburned shoulders. She told them she was up visiting her dad, then pointed to me and said, 'She's a runaway.'

"They seemed kind of impressed, but I didn't like the way she made such a big deal over me. By then, running away wasn't anything I was proud of. So what if I knew how to eat from goddamn garbage cans? By then, I would have done anything to change that, but it was too late. I'd learned to survive too well. For me it was sort of like a trial to stay up there in a real house, sleep in a bed, take food out of a refrigerator, and cook whenever I felt hungry.

"Soon Annie was carrying on a conversation with the boys that should've been copied into one of those books written to help girls pick up guys. She was a fucking master at it.

"'Don't you ever get bored living up here?' she asked. 'I mean does *anything* exciting ever happen?'

"The guy called Sam shrugged. 'It's not so boring with summer people like you messing about.'

"'How do you know we're summer people?'

"''Cause you're sitting out here on the fucking sidewalk.'

"'Well, so are you,' Annie giggled.

"'Say, have you girls ever been to Gifford's Falls?'

"Annie lit a cigarette and smiled. 'Where's that?'

"'It's not far. We can take you if you want. We always go for a swim after work.'

"Annie agreed before I had time to say anything. I wasn't used to meeting guys that way. Usually, I hooked up with someone late at night when we were both too drunk or stoned to give a shit about what we did.

"We followed their pickup along a winding road where the trees became thick and tall, and Annie asked what I thought.

"'About what?'

"'I think Eric likes you.'

"'Which one's Eric?'

"'Shit. What's wrong with you? Haven't you been paying attention to anything? These boys aren't just taking us for a swim. I doubt there's even a place called Gifford's Falls.'

"That's when I reminded her about the relationship she was supposed to be having with my dad, but she pretended she didn't hear. 'I'll take Sam, and you take Eric.'

"'Take him for what?'

"She shrugged. 'I don't know. Whatever.'

"Just then, the pickup pulled off to the side and we drew up behind it. There was a narrow path leading down a steep slope to a thin embankment, and then the rushing river. The boys were already at the shore, stripping down to their boxers. Annie gave me a nudge. 'See. They're real gentlemen. They're not even going to make us look at their hairy asses.' Then she removed her dress and called to me. 'Come on. Don't spoil the fun.'

"I unzipped my shorts and took off my shirt, but kept my underwear on. My body was embarrassing. Ever since I started visiting her, I'd been gaining weight from all those regular meals; the plates of spaghetti and meatballs and pizza we ate up at the house.

"Annie and the boys were laughing in the middle of the rapids as they tried swimming upstream. I wasn't used to swimming, so I dove under once just to see how it felt. The water went right up my nose, and I quickly made it to shore. Eric followed.

"'I don't really like to swim,' I told him when he asked why I got out.

"'Too bad. This is the freshest water in the state.'

"I glanced out to the river and saw Annie and Sam splashing each other and having fun. With a joint or a beer, maybe I could've been entertained too, but I just felt numb. I didn't even know why I was there except Annie wanted me to be with her. By then it was too late to turn back. As if reading my mind, Eric went to the pickup and brought back a six pack. When Sam and Annie got out of the river, we all sat around the logs, drinking beer and watching the water flow downstream.

"'Won't your dad be worried if you don't go home for supper?' Sam asked. The sun was setting, and a pale yellow light sifted through the ferns above.

"Annie giggled. 'Oh Daddy lets me do whatever I want.'

"He moved closer to her. 'And what do you want to do?' he asked.

"'I don't know. I can't think of anything right now,' she teased.

"Eric was inching nearer to me too. When Annie first pointed him out, I hadn't thought he was very cute, but after a few beers I guess I was able to appreciate him more. He wasn't tall, but had these strong arms and a wide chest; not gaunt and bony like the boys I usually hung around. He sounded like the type of guy who could really protect me; he had a job, a car, and seemed to have some money.

"As the evening came on, we all moved up to the pickup. Annie and Sam took the cab while Eric and I lay in the back and covered ourselves with a blanket. The truck was already rocking from whatever Annie and Sam were doing, but Eric was polite. He didn't jump on me, so we just stayed there looking at the stars.

"'Do you ever wonder what else is out there?' he asked, gazing up at the sky.

"'You mean like UFOs?'

"'No. Like here on Earth. I mean, I've been living in this goddamn town all my life, and I know everyone and everything here. I want to find out what it's like not to have a fucking home, or truck, or be able to go out and buy a six-pack at the end of the day, or watch cable TV at night.

"'You mean watch network TV instead?' I joked.

"'You know what I'm talking about. You ran away. There must have been something you ran away *from*.'

"'Shit. People don't choose to run away. I did it because I *had* to. It was impossible to live with my mother and her dumb-ass husband one minute longer. They found me once and tried to put me into rehab, as if that would change me. They said they loved me, but they only loved me because they thought they had to, like the way people believe in Jesus even though deep down they know it's all a crock of shit.'

"'At least they said they love you.'

"'I don't give a damn about that. Love is stupid. Anyone can say it. What they really mean is: 'I want *you* to love *me*.'

"Eric curled up and put his arm around me. I was still looking up at the sky. 'I'll tell you a secret,' he whispered. 'Even Sam doesn't know this. I've saved up enough money. After this summer, I'm getting the hell out of this town. Going away.'

"'Where to?'

"He thought for a moment, as if he were making up his mind right there. Then he said, 'Thailand. I've done some reading. They're Buddhist over there. You know, peaceful people, and it's halfway around the world, a long way from here. I want to get as far away as possible.'

"Suddenly, I had this vision. You know how it is when your mind just snaps and everything becomes clear. I was going to go with him. When he left, I'd be on that plane too.

"Neither one of us really had enough money for the trip, but we fell in love with the idea. I guess we used to fuck to consummate our dream. But when we got here, he turned all weird on me. He got into the Buddhism and meditation crap, and I was just interested in being practical. We needed money. We needed to survive. *I'd* been the runaway.

"Not long after we got to Chiang Mai, I met a guy named Mike. He wasn't like all the other spaced-out travelers. He was actually living in Thailand and had a business going. He said he was looking for someone new in town who wouldn't be recognized. Back in San Francisco, I'd sold some pot and pills, so dealing his shit was easy. My first job was selling some weed down at Crasy Horse, and in ten or fifteen minutes, I got rid of everything. In a few weeks, I was making lots of baht and keeping the shit in my room."

"Did Eric know?" I asked.

Cara shook her head.

Juliette looked skeptical. "And so you didn't tell him you were dealing?"

"He said he'd been set up by the Thai police," I reminded her.

Cara reached for her black velvet bag and took out a syringe and rubber tubing she used to tie her arm off. "I never told him. One day, I came back to the guesthouse. It was afternoon. The sun was so hot, the heat felt like it was going to bust open my skull. All I wanted to do was stick my face into the barrel of water outside the toilets. Our guesthouse was kind of a pit. Whenever I told anyone we were staying there, they felt sorry for me. But it was fucking cheap. Only sixty baht a night. I guess you get what you pay for."

"You mean Tara House?" Juliette asked.

Cara grimaced. "You know the dump?"

"Wasn't it always being raided by the police?"

"Yeah, but I didn't know that. So that afternoon I was coming home and saw all these *farangs* standing outside, staring up at the building as if the image of Buddha had just appeared on the wall. I went up and asked someone what happened, and they told me that the police had gone in and taken a bunch of travelers away."

"And one of them was Eric?" I asked.

"I didn't think so. Why the fuck would the police want anything to do with him? He was a nobody. By then he was kinda like a freak. He kept to himself with all his meditation and chanting. Some people bring home souvenirs from a foreign country; he was going to bring back a whole new lifestyle.

"I started to go up to my room, but the Thai workers were looking at me as if I'd sprung horns on my forehead. Usually they weren't so rude. I'd even sold a few joints to the bartender. He was probably the one who turned me in. Then, just as I reached my floor, I saw that our door was open, and I thought: fucking Eric. You see, we weren't getting along. I figured that he was so lost in his karma shit that he forgot to lock the door. But as I got closer, I noticed that the room looked as though a tornado had just blown through. That's when I realized it was all much worse than I imagined. I searched for my boots where I kept the stash. Usually, they were buried beneath my knapsack, but I couldn't find them. The worst part was, the night before, Mike had brought me down some shit to sell.

"This weird feeling came over me, like I was a helium balloon cut loose, floating up in the sky, looking down onto this giant wreck that was my room. And do you know the whole time I didn't even think about Eric? I just figured he was out ringing bells at some temple or down on his knees kissing the floor of a shrine, but then one of the workers was at the door. That's when I knew something was really wrong. They never came upstairs near a *farang's* room. He was the one who told me that the police had taken Eric away."

"*C'est un cauchemar,*" Juliette whispered.

Cara shrugged. "That was two years ago."

"And you never told anyone?" Juliette asked. Her eyes had been closed, but now they were wide open and flashing.

"Fuck no. I would've been thrown in jail. Besides, I thought it was better if I stayed free. At least that way I could try to get him out."

"Surely, you are joking," Juliette sniffed. "Who do you think you are? Houdini?"

"He could have escaped," Cara insisted. "The timing wasn't right. Then I sort of got wrapped up in things." She nodded to me. "I went to live up in Fang."

Juliette winced and reached for her pipe.

"That's so fucked up," I told her. "How can you keep acting like nothing's happened when he's locked away because of you?"

Cara frowned. "It's not because of me. It was just chance. Fate. That's all."

Juliette shook her head. "Do not tell me about chance. I know about chance. Chance is when something happens for no reason at all, like me getting sick."

Cara glared at her. "That was about as random as the stars coming out at night. You got sick because you fucked diseased men."

Juliette reached into her bag and pulled out her tarot cards. "Let me read your cards."

Cara brushed them away. "I don't believe in that shit. Even if I did, I wouldn't want to know."

"It's just a guide," Juliette argued.

Cara held up her works and started cooking some dope. "This is my guide."

I watched Juliette lie back and close her eyes. She'd become so frail. Even after only a few tokes, the opium had strong hallucinogenic effects. Cara reached for my arm, but I pulled it away. "What's she going to do? Die here?" Cara asked.

"She's going back to France," I whispered, and Cara grinned, as if she wanted to be the last traveler remaining in Thailand.

The bad omens began soon after that. Cara and I lay low in Buak Hat Park waiting for *farangs* to come buy our dope. It seemed as if too many people at the guesthouse knew who we were and what we were doing, so we decided to try a new location. Even sitting hidden under the twisted branches of a leafy bush, I kept having these flashes that something was about to go wrong. Sometimes, while living in the city, I would hear a siren wailing from far away and think that an ambulance was coming for me. I knew if I told Cara about my premonitions, she'd think I was being paranoid, so I kept my worries to myself, hoping I was wrong.

"When was the last time you saw Eric?" I asked her.

"Don't try to convince me to start visiting him again," she warned. "I used to feel guilty about it. I don't anymore."

"Does Mike know?"

"They all know. They're the ones who wanted to get him out. They were afraid he'd tell what he knew about us. But I was good. He never knew a thing."

"Why'd you stop visiting him?"

"He didn't need me anymore. He had someone else."

"Who?"

She looked at me and took a deep breath. "You. Once I saw you talking to him, giving him the attention he need-ed, I knew I was free. I guess I should have thanked you."

When I looked up, I saw the sky had become overcast. I had other questions for her, but a Caucasian couple had sat down on the bench across the way. I didn't know what to make of them, but they made me nervous. Whenever I glanced over in their direction, one or the other would nod and smile, as if they were sending us some kind of cryptic signal. Suddenly, I was certain they were undercover agents. That's when I grabbed Cara and started pulling her up off the ground.

"What's the problem?" She tugged back.

"I think we should go. Those guys over there are narcs."

Cara shook me off her and sat back down. The smell of silt and mud came up off the canal that wound through the city like a water moccasin. Whenever the air turned heavy, we were quickly reminded that the murky water was not far away.

"Watch this," Cara whispered as she got up and strut-ted over toward the strangers. That's when I realized that the last thing I should have done was make her feel as though she were being challenged, because Cara thrived on beating the odds.

I watched as she spoke to the couple, her hands deep inside the pockets of her cut-off jeans, her body swaying side to side. I knew what she was saying because I'd heard the routine a hundred times before and I'd learned it too. First, she'd ask them for a cigarette. Then she'd want to know what country they were from. By the time she told them she'd been living in Chiang Mai for two years, they trusted her completely. After all, weren't we all looking for familiarity to make us feel as if somehow we belonged in that strange land? Once she charmed them with her comradery, she waited until they mentioned drugs. Almost everyone did.

From beneath my sunglasses I observed her as the couple moved to one side to allow Cara to sit down. They made the usual mumblings as they conversed in English. The man and woman claimed they were from Austria, but I didn't believe a word of it. They said they'd been in Chiang Mai for two days and were planning to leave within twenty-four hours. They only came for two weeks and had left a young son with his grandparents outside Vienna. Cara smoked one of their European cigarettes; the kind I was sure had been planted by Interpol to create an aura of authenticity.

The next thing I knew, she was motioning for me to bring over the knapsack. They were going to make a buy and we sold them four bags of smack, nothing unusual. When the deal was complete, we moved away. I kept looking around, expecting the police to come and surround us, but it never happened. Pretty soon we were back at Shangri-La where we spent the rest of the evening getting stoned and playing Boggle with the desk clerk.

Two days later, I read in the *Bangkok Post*—whose

headlines were always filled with the catastrophes that befell Western travelers—that two Austrian tourists were in serious condition at the local hospital after buying bad heroin in Chiang Mai.

Cara never read the papers and wouldn't have heard a thing, so I ran over to her room, the ending flipping through my mind: the grand finale to my travels culminating with me behind bars. When I got there, she was asleep and made an unhappy face when she saw me. I shook the newspaper in front of her eyes. "Something's wrong. You better get up. We need to talk."

She didn't bother reading more than the headlines, but the blood drained from her face as the information sunk in. Then she shrugged. "That shit wasn't bad. It was too good."

"But they got it from us. We almost killed them."

"The stuff must have been nearly pure. Mike cuts it before giving it to me, but I never know by how much." Then she grinned mischievously. "Makes me kind of curious, don't you think? We haven't tried any, have we?"

I wanted to tell her to forget about me, but my lips were already quivering. I knew it was going to be fantastic. I wasn't even hooked, but I was practically hyperventilating just thinking about it. "I'm not shooting up," I told her.

She looked annoyed. "You don't know what you're missing."

Cara lit a candle, then cooked up a spoon of dope over the flame. Her syringe sucked up the bubbling liquid, like a snake drinking up its own venom. When the needle hit her skin, she sank back onto the bed, probably anticipating that speck of time when the world became beautiful again. I did a line or two, and, like a giant eye, I waited as the darkness opened up to gleaming light. Soon, I was floating, buffeted on a pillow of clouds, transported to another land where everything was *pure*. "Pure." That word kept echoing in my mind: pure like the iridescence of water, like the gleam of silver, like fresh fallen snow, like light. I bathed in it, strings of diamonds descending from the sky.

But soon the shadows came in. As the high faded, the sense of euphoria went away too, and I sat slumped on Cara's bed feeling cold and sweaty. My jaw ached and my head was heavy, but I turned just in time to see Cara crawling like a crab across the concrete floor, some kind of liquid gushing from her mouth. The air became rancid. Once I caught sight of her like that, I began retching too. I didn't even have time to look for something to be sick in. I just added to the vomit already on the ground.

She was shaking, her eyes closed, and I knew I had to do something quickly. I hated her for making me feel I needed to help her. She reminded me of a dog I once saw run over in the street. It lay there yelping and twitching, but no one wanted to come to its aid because the creature looked so ugly.

I couldn't ignore her. I wasn't a medic, but she could have been dying. The smells of the room became overwhelming, and I began to gag again. When my puking subsided, some protective instinct came over me. I pulled the sheets off the bed and threw them on top of her. The next thing I knew, I'd covered her with my body to stop her trembling. Her clothes were damp from sweat and vomit, but it didn't matter. It took all my strength just to hug her tightly, until her convulsions stopped and she started breathing regularly again.

When I woke up, we were still on the floor. Cara's eyes were open and she was staring at the wall. She wasn't dead. That was important. But she wasn't fully conscious either. Summoning enough strength, she lifted her head and looked around. "Now this place really is a shit hole," she groaned.

I raised myself high enough to grab some towels and started on my hands and knees, trying to wipe up the mess.

"Never mind cleaning. I'm getting out of this dump anyway."

"You can't leave it like this."

"Why not? Someone will mop it up."

I pulled myself up to the bed and collapsed onto the mattress. "If you check out of here, where are you going to go?"

"I could move in with you," she said.

"You're kidding, right?"

But she shook her head. "It'll be cheaper for both of us."

That was a very bad idea. I needed to get farther away from her, not closer. But on the other hand, if we split the rent, it would only take me half as long to save the money to leave. "You'd have to find somewhere else to keep the shit," I told her.

She looked at me as if I'd just said something completely inconceivable. "What's the use of paying for a room if I have to rent another place for the dope?"

It was the scorn in her voice that reminded me that I couldn't really trust her. She didn't want me to protect myself, because she never protected herself. I couldn't want safety, because she didn't want it, and I knew that that kind of balance would always keep any friendship we had in jeopardy.

I never thought I really had a habit, but at about that time I was beginning to notice I felt like shit when I wasn't high. Weed helped for a while, but in comparison to dope, it was like drinking soda to quench your thirst. Thailand meant very little to me anymore. The country was just a piece of land far enough away from home and anyone who cared what I was doing.

For the first time since I was sixteen, I didn't have a boyfriend, or any male I was close to. Having a relationship with more than one person seemed like an unbearable effort. Whenever someone came up to talk to me, I wouldn't even try to get to know them. I guess I thought by then my life was too impossible to explain.

Sometimes, in the early evening before we went out, Juliette would join us on the balcony outside our room. She was getting thinner. Her energy seemed to have stabilized at some low but functional level. While sitting out there waiting for the heat to dissipate, she listened to us talk about where we'd been and how much we needed to sell that night, and she'd shake her head. "Why is it you never get caught? You practically run your business for everyone to see."

"We're too smart," Cara boasted. "Besides, we don't sell enough to make people suspect."

"Maddy told me you sold the junk to those Austrians who OD'd."

Cara snickered. "So what? Do you know how many *farangs* OD each year? Maybe if we were the only dealers in town it would make a difference, but the police know that if they pick us up, there are hundreds of others out there who'll just take our place."

"I always thought dealing was so dangerous," Juliette admitted. "Now look at me. Isn't it funny? I am the one who picked the truly dangerous profession."

I looked out at the ink-smudged sky, unable to imagine losing her. Her presence seemed like a marker buoy that was slowly slipping out of sight in rough seas.

After the sky turned dark, Cara and I picked ourselves out of our chairs and got ready for business. It didn't take much. Basically, we wanted to look like two travelers stopping in at a bar for an evening of fun. That meant washing up and finding clean clothes: T-shirts and shorts, or a dress. Nothing native like sarongs and flip-flops. We wore those around the guesthouse, as though we'd already stepped off into a place called Oblivion; a spot neither Thais nor Western tourists had marked on their maps.

That night we stopped at La Bamba, a traveler bar we never went to unless it was to sell dope. The music was loud and throbbing. On the dance floor a bunch of *farangs* were jumping around like fleas in a strobe-induced frenzy. That's when I noticed Juliette's old boyfriend, the Thai who used to slip around the guesthouse. I'd always been curious about him. His face was angular and bold, as if he had Indian or Malay blood in him. His long black hair was tied back in his usual red-and-white bandana. Since I knew he was skittish, I approached carefully. I wanted to tell him about Juliette and see if he'd go over to the guesthouse to cheer her up.

He appeared mildly surprised to see me, but nothing a Westerner did ever really surprised a Thai. "I know you," I said, moving a little closer to him so he could hear me over the music. "Aren't you Juliette's friend?"

He didn't say yes or no, but his black eyes seemed to acknowledge that he recognized who I was too.

"Don't you remember me? I lived next door to her at Shangri-La."

He looked down and poked the ashes of his cigarette around in a small ceramic dish.

"She's very sick."

"I'm sorry," he said quietly. "But why do you tell me this?"

"She could die and you could be sick too."

He shook his head. "There's nothing I can do for her. It is how it has to be."

"I'm trying to take care of her until she goes home."

He smiled and started to turn away. "That's very good for you. I hope it works."

"But you don't understand," I called after him. "You should get tested."

"Thank you, but I have nothing to worry for."

I walked back to the table, wishing the music, and the flashing lights, and everyone having such a fucking good time would just disappear. I needed to clear my head. I'd only been living with Cara a short while, but her personality seemed to overwhelm me.

When I returned to our table, she was deep in conversation with a *farang* named Billy. By the way they were talking, I assumed she was finalizing some kind of deal. He said he was an American who came from Boston. He looked like he was still in his teens—clean shaven, with rosy cheeks—but his appearance was deceiving. When I sat down, Cara explained that he'd just gotten back from Vietnam. "He says it's really cheap there. Maybe we should go sometime."

"You can get dinner and a bottle of homemade beer for something like twenty-five cents," Billy added.

Cara's eyes twinkled. I'd never really seen her lit up about a guy. "How long are you staying?" she asked him.

"Thailand's not the same. There are too many Europeans. I hitchhiked all over Vietnam and didn't see one white face, then I come here and it's as if I'm on the Champs Élysées."

"Did you ever feel weird about being an American in Vietnam?" I asked.

He shook his head. "People were really happy to see me. It was as if the war never happened."

"That's funny, because we know some vets who can't stop talking about the war," I told him.

"Yeah. Before I left for the countryside, I met a group of Americans over in Ho Chi Minh City. They said they were on a remembrance tour and looked as if they'd just finished bawling their eyes out."

"Shit. That's stupid," Cara grumbled.

"They were traumatized," Billy told her. "Our country's never given them the respect they deserve."

I knew this remark would bother her. She hated people feeling sorry for themselves.

"How long have you been away?" I asked him.

Cara's eyes widened when he told us he'd been traveling for over three years. "Well, where'd you start out?" she asked, as if it were a challenge for him to recount a story that was even more extreme and exciting than her own.

"Afghanistan. From there I hitched all over India and flew to Kathmandu."

"India must have been amazing. I really wish I could get over there," Cara said, then turned to me, probably hoping to get rid of me for a while. "I thought you wanted to dance."

I shook my head. "I'm tired now."

"I know what you need," she offered, winking playfully.

Billy understood too. "I had some great shit in Nepal. If you like dope, you should get up there."

"I want to real bad," Cara sighed, rubbing her arms.

"Hey, do you know where I could get some?" he asked suddenly. "If I could just get enough to sell back home, it would make this whole trip worthwhile."

Cara and I glanced at each other. Billy's question was like an alarm bell going off harsh and loud in a quiet room. Selling small amounts to *farangs* on the street was one thing, but meeting someone who was crazy enough to take the shit through customs was another story. Cara didn't arrange that. The guys would get involved. But first she had to be sure he wasn't a narc. I held my breath as she gave him the once over. Then after a long pause, she asked how much he wanted.

"Enough to make a few thousand bucks. How much could you get me?"

"Aren't you frightened?" I asked. "You could get busted."

He laughed. "I know what I'm doing."

Cara looked impressed and lit a cigarette. It was her way of stalling; just being careful before she gave anything away.

"Do you think he's a narc?" I asked after he got up to use the toilet.

"I don't think he just came off the Ho Chi Minh Trail," she sniffed.

"I bet Jake would know if he's for real or not."

Cara made a face. "That's bullshit. Look what happened to you. The Thais screw them over all the time. Anyway, I'm not going to connect him up until I find out more about him. He's pretty cute, though, don't you think?"

I shook my head. "Not my type."

"Oh, right. You go for the father figures."

"Have fun," I told her. "I'm going back to the room."

I stepped away from the table and walked out onto the quiet streets. I was just tipsy enough to appreciate the stars gleaming through a layer of clouds, and I walked as if I knew what direction I was heading in, even though nothing looked familiar anymore. I was getting used to that.

*A*m I ever going to get out of here? I feel as though I'm having this bad dream where the harder I try to leave, the more obstacles get in my way. Now I know why I've always had a job. Work brings structure. Without structure, I have freedom, and too much freedom means chaos. Ben thought chaos was good; a disruption of events and emotions. He didn't mind not knowing what was going to happen to him next, because he had faith that things would fall into their rightful place. I'm not so sure.

Yesterday, I got as far away from the guesthouse as possible, hoping to find the Botanic Gardens. I wanted to rediscover the beauty that had enchanted me when I first arrived here. Since I'm from the West, I was expecting manicured lawns and sculpted gardens, but I should have known better. In this part of the world, beauty is not found in such obvious places.

I caught a bicycle rickshaw out to the area where the gardens were supposed to be. The driver let me off at a rusted gate where a worn sign marked the park's entrance. The air smelled cool and fresh. The vegetation was overgrown, but luckily the old rainforest remained intact. A stillness, like a fog, hung over everything. There were no more motorbikes rumbling, or car horns honking, nor was there the incessant chiming of bicycle bells.

I strolled down one deserted path after another until I

came to a pond with long white lilies and lotus blossoms sprouting on top of the murky water. Specks of tiny green algae covered the surface between the thick lily pads. I sat down at the edge and ran my hand through the tepid water, feeling the algae and silt slip between my fingers. When I lifted my arm out, it was covered with small bits of green, as if I were wearing a long lace glove dripping with nature.

I remembered walking through Muir Woods, where the soil was so wet and sloshy, I thought I'd been transported to another planet. The damp mentholated air hung in vapors and I'd breathe in deeply thinking about how I was cleansing my lungs, ridding myself of the stagnating feeling of living in one place for too long.

I've always believed in nature and the importance of being connected to other living things, but now I've drifted far away from all that. I'm caught up in something I don't have any control over and can't really explain. If I have one wish, it's to be strong enough to walk away from all of this, but I feel like a spider who's mortally connected to her web. There's absolutely no way I can break loose without having everything collapse on top of me.

I didn't see much of Cara after she met Billy, or maybe that's how I remember it. Some days, she returned to our room to pick up dope or change clothes. She talked about how she and Billy were going to cross into Burma and hook up with the Karen rebels, or how they were going to sail off to Indonesia and become Hindus on Bali. I didn't ask her how she planned to finance those trips, or what she'd do when she ran out of dope. Obviously, she'd survived a long time without me and there wasn't any need to remind her of how tied to certain aspects of our life she really was. It was Billy I was more concerned about. I didn't think he had ever met anyone like her, and I hoped he wouldn't mind getting left behind whenever she got tired of him. But I never should have wasted a moment worrying about him. His agenda was set long before he ever befriended us.

Juliette's parents finally wrote to say they were sending her brother to bring her home. We didn't know how long it would take, but I promised to stay until he got there. As it happened, he arrived a few days later. I was drinking a cup of Nescafé at the picnic table when a Caucasian man in a suit and tie walked up to the reception desk and asked for Juliette Roubillard. The clerk had no idea who he was talking about, but I offered to take him to her.

"*Vous êtes une amie?*" he asked, as he examined me up and down, like I was some kind of mongrel who'd come sniffing up the back of his leg.

I nodded. "I'm the one who wrote your parents."

He laughed. "Your past perfect is very incorrect."

"Well, I only took French in high school."

"*Et voilà,*" he commented with a smirk.

We started to climb the stairs. Although he didn't ask me to, I followed him right to Juliette's door, thinking that maybe she needed a buffer between herself and this arrogant man. He seemed handsome and conceited in some typically French way, and he looked as if he didn't want to waste much time with the trivialities of his assignment. When he got to her room he nodded, as if I were the maid and he expected me to scamper off, but I just stood there. "*Entrez,*" I whispered. "She's probably asleep."

He opened the door, but stopped when he saw how

dark the room was. "It's nearly three in the afternoon," he commented. "Why would she still be sleeping?"

Suddenly, I worried that my French had been so inadequate it didn't express the seriousness of her condition. But then Juliette made some noises and pulled herself up to a sitting position, reaching to open the shutters that blocked out the light. "Charles," she gasped when she saw him.

He went over and greeted her with four swift pecks to the cheek. I could tell by the way he pulled away that he was utterly disgusted by what he saw. Then they started speaking French rapidly, but whatever he was saying didn't sound very comforting to me. He kept flinging his arms around the room, as if he was personally offended by the way she was living. I stepped away and waited on the balcony for him to leave. In less than ten minutes, he was outside again, leaning over the railing smoking a cigarette. "What has happened to her? What have you done? She used to be a beautiful girl, you know."

"She's sick. She's got HIV. SIDA," I tried to explain, but he kept shaking his head.

"How could she? How do you know?"

I looked at him, not quite understanding what he was asking, but he continued. "This is such a filthy country. Why would she leave Paris for this? She had a home and a family. Has she seen a doctor? How does she know she has this thing for sure?"

Just then Juliette appeared from inside the room. She'd dressed herself in baggy sweatpants and a T-shirt, and she held onto both sides of the door frame for support. Her face was gaunt; her eyes flashed angrily. "See," she said glaring at me. "I told you it was useless. He doesn't understand a thing."

Her brother broke in, saying something to her in French. Then he pushed past her and started tearing her room apart, looking for a bag to pack her belongings. By then, she was brushing away tears. In all the conversations we had, she'd always been so strong. I never once saw her cry or feel sorry for herself. "He says he's going to take me to the Westin. He doesn't want me to stay in this guest-house any more. But once they see me like this, they're never going to let me into that hotel. He has tickets for tomorrow afternoon. First we fly to Bangkok, then home to France."

"Can't she stay here one more night?" I asked, turning to Charles. He had found her knapsack and was shoving all her clothes into the worn pouch.

"Why do you need her one more night? So you can kill her? Is it you who has made her this way? What kind of things are you doing to her? People just don't get to be like this. She's only twenty-eight. And you have the nerve to ask if she can stay in this disgusting pit one moment longer?"

I started to back away. He was determined to get her out of there and probably thought that with the same willpower, he could also make her better. Juliette stood holding onto my arm and shaking. I squeezed her fingers tight. "He's going to take you home," I whispered. "That's what you wanted."

She started sobbing even harder. "He doesn't understand. Don't you see?"

"You need a doctor and medicine; more than what they can give you here."

"Oh, I wish I were dead already."

With that, Charles came up and nudged me away. I needed all the restraint in the world to keep myself from shoving him back, but I kept on thinking that anything that prevented Juliette from returning to France was not helping her. The best thing I could do was let her brother take her with him.

When they finally came downstairs, Charles had dressed her in a short cotton skirt and tank top, something she could have worn beautifully when she was healthy, but now it looked like a bad fit on her skeletal frame. She shuffled along quietly, no longer walking confidently on the balls of her feet. Although she'd stopped crying, her eyes and nose were still pink and swollen.

The desk clerk sorted out her bill while Charles stood impatiently, holding his wallet.

"Thank you," she whispered, grabbing my hand. "You've been so beautiful and kind. You took care of me when nobody else would. Whenever I think of a friend, I'll think of you."

I didn't want to start crying too, but then Charles came and stood between us. "Say good-bye," he commanded in French.

Juliette leaned toward me and kissed me on the cheek. As her lips swept by my face, I felt her eyelash brush against my skin, gentle and light, like a wave of a dancer's hand or a quick jeté of nimble feet. When she was gone, I ran up into my room and dug through Cara's things. It wasn't hard to find what I was looking for. She still kept her dope in her black velvet bag. I couldn't leave the world fast enough.

Most tourists take photographs of the places they've been. Disposable cameras, film, and videotape are on sale at souvenir shops all over the world, along with T-shirts and trinkets with emblems to mark the spot in your mind. From Egypt, it could be a ceramic cast of the pyramids or the Sphinx; France, a miniature brass Eiffel Tower; London, a Big Ben piggy bank or Westminster Abbey paperweight. It's funny, but when I look at what I've brought home with me, I have so few physical items to remind me of my trip: no carved elephant or photographs of the Golden Triangle; nothing I can place on my desk or bureau and proudly say, "See, I've been there!"

In the evening, I woke up to find Cara sitting on her bed flipping through a Thai magazine. It was strange to see her so quiet. For once, she wasn't dashing around changing clothes, looking for keys, money, or anything else she'd forgotten.

"You're back," I whispered.

"Juliette's gone," she observed.

"It's so fucked up. Why'd it have to happen to her?"

"Bad luck," Cara said spitefully. "Isn't that what she's always said?"

"Can't you be serious for once?"

"Well, what do you want me to say?"

"Why don't you say you're sorry it happened to her."

"She never felt sorry for me."

"She's probably going to die, and you're just thinking about yourself."

"If it wasn't for me caring about myself and keeping us alive, how long do you think you could have stayed here? You would've left Thailand months ago."

She rustled through her bags, scrounging up a cigarette.

"So, where's Billy?" I asked.

She shrugged. "He's too fucking weird. All he cares about is when I'm going to get his shit for him to take back home. But he's not going home. He doesn't even have an airplane ticket."

"Maybe he's got one waiting for him at the airport."

"I just don't get it. Why the hell isn't he leaving?"

"Have you seen his passport?"

"I've looked for it, but I haven't found one. You know, I don't even think his name is Billy. He always seems surprised when I call him that. Why's he hanging around me? What does he want?"

"Maybe he likes you."

"Why doesn't he like *you*? You're nicer. Why would he want to be with me, if he could have you?"

"Come on."

"You're just saying that because you're some kind of fucking optimist. If the sky was black and full of clouds and I said it was going to rain, you'd find some way to try to convince me that the sun was shining."

"I'm not that bad."

"You should listen to yourself. 'And then Prince Charming put the slipper on Cinderella's foot and it fit perfectly.' If you want to know, I snuck out of his room tonight. I told him I needed some time to breathe. I feel like I'm under surveillance. He won't let me out of his sight."

"You've practically been with him ever since you met."

"Maybe I'm paranoid, but he seems pretty uptight for some laid-back traveler."

"You probably make him nervous."

"Fuck you. I'm as calm as the next person."

"Now that Juliette's gone," I began, glancing around

the room, thinking it was as good a time as any to tell her, "I don't know what I'm staying here for."

She squinted at me. It was the look she always gave me when something I said annoyed her. "Why does everything have to be for a reason? Do you always have to have some goddamn purpose?"

"*I* do," I told her.

"Well, what's changed?"

I stared at the concrete walls. "I don't know. I just feel so empty, like I've lost everything, maybe even myself. I used to be this *person* who knew who she was and what she was doing, but now I feel as if me, that old self, has disappeared."

We were quiet for a while as the smoke from a joint swirled around the room. Our clothes lay everywhere, tossed in clumps about the floor. We no longer separated our belongings. I guess those divisions didn't make sense anymore. "What're you going to do if I leave?" I asked her.

Cara smirked. "I can take care of myself."

"Are you going to hook Billy up with the guys?"

She shook her head. "He'll just get us busted. He doesn't know what the fuck he's doing. I'm not going to end up in jail because of him."

The evening began slowly. A strong wind blew up off the river, sending the palm fronds crackling as they whipped against each other in the warm breeze. We started out at La Bamba where only three or four tables were filled with travelers. Not the usual crowd. Maybe everyone figured the unsettled weather was going to bring rain, although the monsoons had swept through months before.

Cara and I ordered beers, nothing too strong, and stared at the strobe light rotating against the empty dance floor. "Where is everybody?" she asked. "It's as if the Thais have evacuated the whole city. If this keeps up, we'll have to find some place else to hang out." Then, she got up to buy some cigarettes.

I knew she wasn't going to be gone long, so I sat back and listened to the shrill Thai singing coming from the loudspeakers. The traditional music reminded me of Jake and all the rides we'd taken into the countryside. I missed him and his way of exploring the pockets of Thailand that tourists rarely saw. I wondered where he was and how I'd remember him when I got back home. Already, I was experiencing the anesthetic effects of memory and travel, where the bad parts were forgotten and only good bits remained.

Then Billy was standing in the entranceway. Something about the way he came striding toward me made him stick out. My knees automatically locked around the knapsack, as if the bag were a physical part of my body that I needed to protect. I was beginning to think that maybe Cara wasn't being paranoid and there really *was* something strange about him.

"How you doing?" he asked, sliding into the chair next to me.

"Cara went to get some cigarettes," I told him.

He was dressed weirdly in stiff new Levis and a white T-shirt neatly tucked into his pants. Most travelers had worn out their Western clothing by the time they reached Chiang Mai. He put his hand into his pocket and opened up a shiny black leather wallet. I thought he was going to offer to buy me a drink, but he flashed the wallet on the table and started talking as if there was something inside that I should have seen. For a few seconds I didn't understand, but then I followed his gaze down and saw that he was showing me some kind of U.S. government ID.

"Is that a sheriff's badge?" I joked.

In answer, he grabbed the knapsack from beneath the table and pulled me up by my elbow, dragging me outside into a nearby alleyway. I prayed for Cara to return, but Billy had already pushed me into the shadows and was holding me against a wall. "This isn't a game. You've got to act smart. In three minutes the police are going to be here and raid this place. They don't give a shit about you. Just answer their fucking questions, and you'll be on a plane back to the States."

At first I didn't understand. "What about Cara?" I asked.

"Let them take care of her."

"But what are they going to do?"

He squeezed my arm tighter. "She's not going to die. Just go back into that room and sit there like you're fucking waiting for her."

He held the knapsack out for me to take, but I shook my head. "Please. It's not mine. I didn't bring it."

"Jesus, don't act stupid. We know all about you. You're not the one we want." Then he curled my fingers around the strap and pushed me back into the bar. I didn't want to go, but he gave me a shove. With each step, my body seemed to weaken. My limbs started shaking until I could hardly hold myself together. Billy came up behind me and led me back to my seat, then placed the knapsack on the ground where it had been before. I had no idea how much stuff was still in there. We usually sold what would be considered dime bags for a few hundred baht, but we hadn't sold anything that night.

I waited for what felt like hours, but really it was only a few minutes. When Cara came into the room, she was smiling broadly, flicking ashes from her cigarette onto the floor. "Guess who I just saw? The boys are back in town," she sang. "Isn't that funny? They're coming in to have a drink."

My tongue was heavy. I barely managed to swallow the saliva that was accumulating at the base of my lower lip. She looked at me strangely. We hadn't been friends very long, and I didn't think she was too perceptive, but I knew she could tell something was wrong. "Shit, you look sick. I thought you'd be happy to see them," she laughed.

I shook my head, thinking about Jake, Mike, and Pete walking into that trap and wishing I knew how to harness the power of the mind and move us back in time so we could all escape whatever was about to happen. Then there was a strange silence, the way there is before a hurricane or tornado. Everything stood still. The wind stopped blowing. Cara stopped talking. It even seemed as if the lights on the dance floor were no longer spinning. I was trembling so badly, I thought I was going to have some kind of fit; the kind where your brain just seizes from being overloaded with too much stimuli. The only image I could focus on was Billy's face as he forced me against the wall and snarled something about going home. That's when I knew I had to do whatever I could to save myself.

I started crying the moment I saw the uniforms. Cara looked at me. Her eyes were hard and spiteful. She thought I'd turned her in, but I hadn't. If there was anything I could have done to protect us, I would have tried, but it was too late. One of the policemen grabbed me. Someone else took the knapsack. Billy was nowhere to be seen.

They split us up. I was put in a dark van where an American was in charge. He shouted orders to a Thai commander who then yelled at the uniformed men. Outside, the sky was black. The trees were still swaying madly in the wind. Somehow, we had moved into another street, and I recognized the three dirt bikes parked in a row. I knew who they belonged to and started crying even harder. The last thing I wanted was for Jake to see me like that, but they must have already taken him away.

The van started up again, and sometime afterward, we arrived at a small house outside the city. I remember thinking it was nearly dawn because a thin streak of light swept low across the horizon. One of the Thai policemen led me and began jabbering in heavily accented English. He asked me all kinds of questions. I knew I shouldn't answer him, but I kept remembering what Billy had said about going home.

At first I thought he'd ask about Cara, but he said he already knew about her. The person who called himself Billy had told them everything he'd learned. They wanted to know about Mrs. Chang, Lek, Mike, Pete, and Jake. As they interrogated me, I kept wishing I hadn't begged Jake to tell me all about what they were doing. All that time I thought he was hiding something from me because he didn't trust me. Now I knew he was also trying to protect me. Whatever was going to happen to him was going to be a thousand times worse than what was happening to me.

Someone brought me a cup of tea. Although the American spoke more gruffly, I felt safer talking to him, as if our common nationality shielded me. "It's the Thais' call," he told me. "If they have enough information and you're just small potatoes, they might put you on a plane at Don Muang. If not, you were carrying a moderate quantity of an illegal substance. They could prosecute you to the fullest extent of the law."

"But what does that mean?" I practically screamed.

He pinched the skin on his forehead. "Maybe eight to fifteen?"

"But it wasn't even mine!"

"Look. I'm going to do you a favor and tell you one thing: forget about it. You were in possession of an illegal substance. Even though your name isn't written on every speck, you were in possession and it's yours!"

"Don't I get a lawyer?"

He grinned. "That depends on if they charge you."

"So you think they might not?"

Three Thai policemen came in and the American quickly moved aside. I looked at the dirt floor and continued to whimper. Except for the tea, I hadn't eaten anything since the previous afternoon and bubbles of nausea kept rising from the pit of my stomach.

The Thai policeman approached again. I could tell by his face that he was disgusted at the way I was behaving. To him, I was an irritation, someone who stood between him and his real prey. He'd gone to the guesthouse to search my room, and he now held my backpack upside down, dumping everything out on the floor. All my belongings lay in front of me in a heap: my shirts and shorts, dresses and underwear, swimsuit, books, and diary. Everything there. Then he waved my passport in my face. "We already know about your friends. You work with us and there's no problem, no arrest, no prison. You go home and we no see you again. You no work with us, you stay in Thailand long time. You be our guest in Thai jail."

"What do you want to know?" I shuddered.

There was a silence, and the Thai man shook his head. "We will come to you when it's time."

I turned to the American who was standing in the back of the room. Already the sunlight was spilling in through the cracks in the wooden walls. It was going to be another goddamn glorious day and I wouldn't know a thing about it. "What about me?" I begged. "How long will I be here?"

"You'll go where they take you and cooperate if that's what they want," the American replied.

"Am I going to jail?"

The Thai shook his head. "No jail. You stay here. We be back tomorrow."

He started walking out into the daylight, into the heat, into the blue sky and freedom, into everything I'd taken for granted for so many months. The rest of his men followed. Then the American came up to me. "I'm sorry I can't do more, but this is their country. You should get some sleep. You'll feel better when you wake up."

My eyes were watering and my nose had started running. "I feel like shit right now," I complained.

"I know. Kicking is going to be the hardest part."

I remember thinking he was crazy. I wasn't hooked, so there was nothing to kick. "What about the others? What's going to happen to them?"

"You're in enough trouble on your own. Don't worry about them." Then he started walking out of the room toward the van.

"Who are you with anyway?" I called after him. "Interpol? The CIA?"

He looked back and smiled a toothy grin of someone who has nothing to hide. "DEA. Special Agent Breen."

"You don't think they're going to send me to jail?" I yelled hopefully, but he just shook his head and kept walking toward the door.

"Sleep well," I heard him say.

Through the slats in the walls, I saw him get into the van, then I heard the noise as it pulled out from the gravel. At first I thought I was alone. No one seemed to be near the hut, but as I peeked outside the door, I saw two Thai policemen had been left with me and were sitting quietly on wooden stools. When they noticed I was there, they quickly waved me back inside.

I had no idea what time it was that awful day. I watched the sun move along the cracks from behind the walls. At one point, the guards started talking, their voices rising, light and flirty. When I peered out, I saw they were speaking to a young girl who'd brought over a pot of sticky rice and chicken curry. The guards took theirs first and gave the rest to me. I didn't feel hungry, but I was weak and knew I should try to eat. At first I thought they hadn't given me a spoon or chopsticks because of some kind of prison rule, but then I remembered seeing other Thais eat with their fingers up north, and I closed my eyes, squeezing them shut and wishing I was back in the countryside riding with Jake, my cheeks chapped and stinging from all the wind and sun, my mind free, my thoughts on simpler things. But when I opened my eyes again, I was still in that house, listening to the insects hit the walls.

I was kept there for three days with nothing to take my mind off what was happening to me or what had become of Cara and the others. Sometimes, I wished I was with them, not set apart and feeling guilty knowing that my natural instinct was to save myself and give them away.

The Thai guards changed every twelve hours. That's how I knew how much time had passed. The same girl brought food once a day, and the guards occasionally made tea on a small fire. They seemed to be suffering nearly as much as I was because they were forced to sit outside where the heat and flies were the worst.

On the third day, a vehicle pulled up. Its wheels crunched along the dirt, then stopped. The doors opened and closed. Then footsteps marched toward the house. By then I was a mess. My brain was tangled with scenarios of what was going to happen to me and the many mistakes I'd made that had gotten me into such a situation in the first place. I didn't know who I hated more: Jake and Cara for luring me into their business, or myself for never standing up and leaving Chiang Mai before it was too late.

This time, only the Thai official and Agent Breen entered the room. I'd been continuously sweating. When I wasn't sweating, I was shivering and my flesh felt as if it were being bitten by hundreds of fire ants. It was hard to even pretend that I was normal, so I gave up and let the tremors take over.

"Madeline Foster," Agent Breen began, ignoring the way I was clinging to one side of the wall, cowering like some frightened beast.

I nodded, but didn't know why he was speaking to me in such a formal tone. "You are being released. We have authorization to transport you to Bangkok's Don Muang airport where you are to board American Airlines flight 721 to Los Angeles International Airport."

I flew into his arms, but he quickly pushed me away. "How'd it happen? Why are they letting me go?"

He sighed long and hard, as if to emphasize his boredom with my case. "They're not after you, simple as that. If they busted every *farang* who had dope in Thailand, the jails would be even more full of Westerners than they already are. The same night they got you, they took in your friends. You were brought in with the dirt as they swept up."

I thought of Jake, Mike, Pete and Cara and started to cry all over again, but the Thai shook his head unhappily. "Come on. You go now."

I looked down at my knapsack where I'd carefully folded all the clothes, some mine, some Cara's. In those three days, I was able to organize the mess. Shirts lay with shirts, dresses with dresses, shorts and underwear were piled together. Even though I could have left the clothes there, I wanted to keep them with me, hoping their smell and texture would remind me of what had happened. Then I took my journal, which filled two notebooks. The papers' edges were wrinkled and waterlogged. Bits of sand and dirt fell from inside the spine, but every page was filled with my curving script, documenting my days and months in Thailand. All that time I spent writing, I never really knew why I was doing it. Now the diary exists to tell a story I don't want to forget; a story about a time when I was very lost, but not alone; when I made some bad decisions, but something like fate or luck protected me; when I was stupid and naive, but struggled with choices some people will never have to make.

I flew home the next day. Outside the little oval window, the airplane seemed to drift weightlessly above the clouds. I had no idea what was going to happen next, but inside that enclosed environment I felt safe. Nothing changed, only morning seemed to be dawning over and over again.

NAVA RENEK was born in Nyack, New York and raised in the Bronx, Manhattan, and Pound Ridge, New York. After completing her BA in English literature, she lived in various parts of the United States, and traveled extensively in Europe, Southeast Asia, and Mexico. She is an adjunct lecturer, program developer, and grant writer at Brooklyn College, where she received her MFA. Her fiction and non-fiction has appeared in newspapers and literary magazines, most recently in The MacGuffin and The Brooklyn Rail. She lives in Brooklyn with her husband Paul and son Evan. This is her first novel.

Acts of Levitation    Laynie Browne
ISBN 1-881471-94-2    $14.00

Like Scherherazade, Lewis Carroll, or the Shakespeare of the late romances, Browne possesses an ability to dazzle the reader by creating wondrous worlds in which the usual laws of plausibility are suspended. Indeed, her writing is saturated with the echoes, not only of these writers, but of numerous sources derived from the canon of fabulist literature.   —Outlet

The Farce    Carmen Firan
ISBN 1-881471-96-9    $10.00

You can hear in Firan's prose the turning over of the wheel of time, the changing of once seemingly immutable orders, the anguish of people struggling to escape history and to understand themselves. Her writing lifts the curse, briefly.
—Andrei Codrescu

Don't Kill Anyone, I Love You
Gojmir Polajnar
translated from the Slovene
by Aaron Gillies
ISBN 1-881471-80-2   $12.00

Polajnar may become something of a Balkan Irvine Welsh... —Library Journal

ARC: Cleavage of Ghosts     Noam Mor
1-881471-79-9     $14.95

...possibly the most phallocentric protagonist since Philip Roth's Portnoy....the power of Mor's voice is undeniable. —Rain Taxi

6/2/95     Donald Breckenridge
ISBN 1-881471-77-2  $14.00

Fifteen characters travel through New York City on a single day in 1995. Their paths intersect in a finely choreographed Altmanesque dance. —The New Yorker

The Fairy Flag & Other Stories     Jim Savio
ISBN 1-881471-83-7  $14.00

These stories will be appreciated by a wide audience, as they evoke wide ranges of emotion, from the violent to the poetic.
—Foreword

Ted's Favorite Skirt     Lewis Warsh
ISBN 1-881471-78-0   $14.00

The heroine is a hoops-shooting, Madame Bovary reading American kid trying to figure it all out. —Laird Hunt

Little Tales of Family & War     Martha King
ISBN 1-881471-47-0     $12.00

King is a minimalist with a difference. Where much minimalist prose is dry and detached, King's is richly detailed. —American Book Review

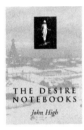

The Desire Notebooks     John High
ISBN 1-881471-33-0  $14.95

...accurately conveyed desire to make a novel tell the story of love and death, always and everywhere. —Publishers Weekly

Black Lace     Barbara Henning
ISBN 1-881471-62-4  $12.00

Detroit circa 1970. Eileen skips out, forsaking any desire she might once have had for a regular family life. Melancholy dominates. Abandonment prevails. —Village Voice

The Poet     Basil King
ISBN 1-881471-69-1     $14.00

Spencil sketches with reminiscences of poets and writers from the early 1980's, including Baraka, Ginsberg, Berkson, Metcalf, Owen, Selby, Auster and others.

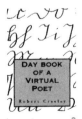

Day Book of a Virtual Poet     Robert Creeley
ISBN 1-881471-28-4     $12.00

Throughout the text, Creeley's enthusiasm never flags... —Wired Magazine

## Other titles from Spuyten Duyvil

*Kaleidoscope 1969*    Joanna Gunderson
*Track*    Norman Finkelstein
*Columns*    Norman Finkelstein
*A Flicker at the Edge of Things*    Leonard Schwartz
*The Long & Short of It*    Stephen Ellis
*Stubborn Grew*    Henry Gould
*Identity*    Basil King
*Warp Spasm*    Basil King
*The Runaway Woods*    Stephen Sartarelli
*The Open Vault*    Stephen Sartarelli
*Cunning*    Laura Moriarty
*Mouth of Shadows: Two Plays*    Charles Borkhuis
*The Corybantes*    Tod Thilleman
*Detective Sentences*    Barbara Henning
*Are Not Our Lowing Heifers Sleeker
Than Night-Swollen Mushrooms?*    Nada Gordon
*Gentlemen in Turbans, Ladies in Cauls*    John Gallaher
*Spin Cycle*    Chris Stroffolino
*Watchfulness*    Peter O'Leary
*The Jazzer & The Loitering Lady*    Gordon Osing
*Apo/Calypso*    Gordon Osing
*In It What's in It*    David Baratier
*Transitory*    Jane Augustine
*The Flame Charts*    Paul Oppenheimer
*Transgender Organ Grinder*    Julian Semilian
*Answerable to None*    Edward Foster
*The Angelus Bell*    Edward Foster
*Psychological Corporations*    Garrett Kalleberg
*The Evil Queen*    Benjamin Perez
*Moving Still*    Leonard Brink
*Breathing Free*    Vyt Bakaitis (ed.)
*XL Poems*    Julius Keleras
*Miotte*    Ruhrberg & Yau (eds.)
*Knowledge*    Michael Heller
*Conviction's Net of Branches*    Michael Heller
*See What You Think*    David Rosenberg

SPUYTEN DUYVIL BOOKS ARE DISTRIBUTED TO THE TRADE BY

Biblio Distribution
*a division of NBN*
1-800-462-6420
www.bibliodistribution.com